QUEEN OF FROST

Frost Book One

ARIA NOBLE

STERLING & STONE

The authors greatly appreciate you taking the time to read our work.
Please consider leaving a review wherever you bought the book, or
telling your friends about it, to help us spread the word.

Thank you for supporting our work.

QUEEN OF FROST

Chapter One

EMBER COULDN'T SEE. She'd been squinting through glare and blizzards, snow and ice, for her entire life, but she'd never been in a whiteout as complete as this. The wind tore into the ground, picking up snow and ice that had already fallen and adding their particles to what was falling, and had been falling, from the sky for three days. When she held her black thermal mitten out in front of her face, it vanished behind a wall of blowing, biting snow, as completely as though she hadn't lifted it at all.

The rope around her waist went slack. She tugged at it, suddenly afraid that something happened at the other end, that it came unknotted from Eli's waist, and they were about to be separated. Half-panicked scenarios starting whirling around in Ember's head.

In storms like this, with whiteouts so bad one can't see their mitten in front of their face, a person could be just steps away from shelter and freeze to death before they could find it. Companions could be lost only feet away from each other.

There was an answering tug on the rope, and Ember

could breathe again. She followed it forward. She could only tell she was moving by the feeling of her boots crunching through the icy crust of the snow. Eli shimmered into view an instant before she ran into him. He stood still, his head and shoulders hunched over. His face was hidden behind a thermal scarf, hat, hood, and goggles, but he appeared to be looking down at something in his hands.

Ember put a mittened hand on his shoulder to let him know she was there and leaned against his arm to see what he was looking at.

It was the compass.

She'd let him take it for a while, mostly because she was tired of being in the lead. They'd been following the compass needle since first setting foot beyond the walls of Dusk, but now it was spinning again.

Ember pressed closer to him so she could speak through scarves and hats and blizzard winds. Even with her head practically shoved against his, she had to shout to be heard over the wind. "We should stop. Let the weather die down."

Eli looked up from the compass. Ember couldn't see his face, but she could hear the frown in his tone. "I think this means we're almost there."

She glanced over her shoulder, though the gesture was useless. She couldn't see anything past the little bubble of space before the falling, blowing snow turned everything to solid white.

The movement in the corner of her eye, the dark shape she thought she saw whenever she wasn't looking at it — she knew it was all in her head. She'd heard of such things happening to people caught in whiteouts, how the lack of visual stimulation could cause them to start seeing things that weren't there. Shadows lurking at the corners of their vision, monsters padding along behind them and disappearing whenever they turned to look directly.

She knew it was because she'd spent the last who knew how long trying to see a world that was completely wiped away, but the feeling of something following them, the momentarily glimpses of the shadows lurking in her vision, still frightened her.

"Eli, please. Let's stop. The weather's been getting worse since morning, and I'm tired."

She hated to admit it, but it was true. Her body ached with the effort of walking across the knee-deep, ice-crusted snow, and her head ached from trying to see through the walls of white that pressed in around her like a shifting cocoon.

"Okay," Eli agreed. It would be unthinkable of him to argue with her plea. Tired equaled dead out here. "The next drift we find, we'll dig in for a rest."

It took only a few minutes to stumble across a suitably large drift; they were common on the lee side of every bump and mound of the ground out here. This one was as tall as Eli's head, and though they had to break through the crust of ice on the top of it to make their opening, they'd soon dug a nook big enough for both of them to fit inside.

It was better inside the drift, out of the wind and away from the blinding blanket of snow. Ember unhooked herself from her pack and pulled off her goggles. The air bit into the exposed flesh around her eyes, but out of the wind and snow, the cold was barely even remarkable, hardly any colder than stepping outside her house at home.

Her goggles were crusted with ice inside and out. She scraped them clean with her mittened hand while Eli wormed his way into the hole and took off his pack and goggles too.

He reached for the layers around his mouth and tugged them away from his face. They had a thin crust of ice on them, too, a crust Ember could feel beginning to melt into her own knitted wool beneath the thermal layer on the outside.

Dusk didn't have much, but it did have thermals. Even Before, Dusk had been so far north that the climate was cold and unpredictable, so a lot of people stockpiled thermals. After the Great Death, thermals became every person's most carefully maintained possessions. Ember had even heard stories, though mostly from Eli, that Frost might be producing them again.

Of course, everything she knew about Frost came from Eli's stories. "Frost has warmth. Light. Even industry," he'd say. Or, "I've heard you can get milk — real milk, like from animals — in Frost. They grow animals down there!"

Did she believe him? On some level, Ember figured she must. Dusk couldn't be the only place that had survived the Great Death, and Frost had been the crown jewel of Steppe Before — or so she'd been told, as neither she nor her parents, or even their parents as far as she knew, were old enough to actually remember it. There *had* to be something beyond Dusk. There *had* to be, and that was why she was here. Why she let Eli talk her into this trip.

Besides, if she didn't come, Eli would die wandering around in the tundra. There was only one real rule about traveling alone outside of Dusk's walls, and that was *don't*.

But Ember knew, as she trudged along through the snow and the whiteout, tugged onward by her own curiosity, that keeping Eli alive and safe wasn't the real reason she'd let him convince her to come. There was something else beneath the rationalizations she gave herself, reasons she didn't fully understand — and that sometimes, like now, began to feel inexcusably stupid.

She was supposed to be the cautious one, the level-headed one, the one who talked Eli out of his wildest ideas and most absurd desires. She wasn't sure how she'd let him talk her into this.

"I think we're almost there." His voice was soft. He no longer needed to shout over the wind and thick layers of clothing.

Ember didn't answer. He'd been saying that since the snow started three days ago.

"Ember?"

"I heard you," she mumbled into her scarf. She kept her eyes on her hands and continued to scrub at her goggles, even though the coating of ice was long gone.

Eli watched her. His gaze pressed into her skull like stones, hard and heavy. Eventually, he sighed and turned to his pack. He pulled out the thermal bag folded and tucked neatly into an inner pocket.

Thermal sleeping bags were things Ember had only ever seen in a store window. The first night Eli had taken it out of his pack, she realized just how long he'd been planning and preparing for this trip: the only thermal bags she'd ever seen cost as much as Eli could make in a year at his job of keeping Dusk's streets clear of the snow and ice that forever threatened to bury their homes beneath the weather.

Now, Eli unrolled the bag. It was thin and matte black like all thermals and just large enough for the both of them to snuggle in together, sharing their body heat as the cloth reflected it back on them. He stretched it out on the hard-packed snow floor of their little cave, then looked up at Ember and grinned with half his mouth. "Bedtime?"

Ember shed her outermost layers, setting the thermals and wool aside to dry, then quickly slid between the two layers of the bag. Eli did the same, and in a couple of minutes, Ember was finally able to feel her toes again.

She wiggled them, relieved when they moved, however painfully, under her command. Snow had slipped into her boots at some point and soaked her socks; she peeled the socks off, knocking Eli with her knee as she pulled it up to reach her foot.

"What was that for?" he asked, shifting away from her accidental kneeing.

"Sorry," she whispered back, then, fighting down a grin, stuck two of her toes against the bottom cuff of his pants, against the warmth she could feel radiating from his leg.

He twitched and yelped as her cold toes connected with his warmer ankle.

Ember bit back a chuckle. For someone who grew up in a place forever covered in snow and frozen in ice, who spent his days trudging through drifts up to his hips or higher, he was surprisingly sensitive to the cold.

Then she sighed. "Almost there, huh?"

He nodded and snuggled down a little further into the bag so that only the top of his head and his mop of over-grown, dusty black hair stuck out. "I'm sure of it. We haven't made great time because of the weather the last couple of days, but you'll see. There's more beyond the tundra." A yawn, wide enough to make Ember's jaw ache just looking at it. "There has to be."

Ember snuggled down, too. Eli was so warm, probably the warmest boy she'd ever met. Dusk tended to make people like her: cold from skin to bone, hardened by life at an age that she felt must be far too young. But Eli had never been like that. Both his body and his demeanor stayed warm to the touch no matter how brutal the weather got, and somehow, through the years, through endless winter nights, the illnesses and accidents that haunted every footstep, the ice and snow that never relented even when the sun came back for the summer, Eli never lost that warmth.

Her father had described him as a candle flame once before he disappeared into the tundra and never came back, and the image had stayed with Ember ever since. Eli was a flame, and she had always been drawn to him.

They were a team, the two of them. Ember kept them smart, and Eli kept them warm.

She must've dozed off because she woke with a start to Eli snoring softly at her back and a pale bluish light coming into their little burrow from the hole where they'd dug into the drift.

Her nerves jangled. Something tugged at her in that deep-down space she had spent a good portion of her life trying to ignore, but that never really went away.

Ember rolled over and prodded Eli in the shoulder. He flopped onto his back, away from her finger, but then opened his eyes.

"G'morning, sleepy," Ember muttered. "It looks like the storm has stopped."

Eli lifted his head to look out from the drift, then settled back against his pack, which he was using as a pillow. His eyes closed again. "Just a few more minutes."

She let him have that. She wasn't in a hurry, after all. This might not even be the worst place to spend the night. They had shelter and a warm thermal bag, and enough ice to suck on when their mouths got dry.

But she couldn't close her eyes. Her attention kept churning over the opening of their little cave and the light outside of it. It was strange. Too blue. It bothered her.

Eli was already snoring again, and he didn't shift when she slid out from the bag. The cold stabbed at her now-warm body, her exposed hands and face and toes, like the very air was made of shards of ice. But that was normal. She slid her feet into her boots and her arms into her coat and scrambled toward the hole in the drift. The ice gathered at the edges was thin enough to break away with her elbows and forearms. She kept her unmittened hands tucked inside the sleeves of her coat. She was just stepping out to see what the strange blue tint to the light was about so she could stop worrying about it and go to sleep, not preparing to walk on — and after a minute of shoving aside some ice and snow, she was able to wiggle her way free of the cave.

The storm had finally stopped, and the wind had whisked away much of the snow, so the ground around their cave was pretty well empty and flat, coated in a thin but treacherous sheet of ice. It was hard to tell with the clouds still so low and thick, but Ember thought by the quality of the gathering darkness that it was coming on evening. For the first time in three days, the air was still. The blueness of the remaining light was diffuse and transparent, but she wasn't sure where it was coming from or why it was there. Everything before her stretched out in near-perfect whiteness for as far as she could see.

Maybe it was like the shadows she'd seen skulking around the corners of her vision during the whiteout. Now that visual information had returned, and her mind was struggling to adjust and colored everything a faint blue that wasn't actually there. Maybe Ember was making something out of nothing again.

She did have a tendency to do that. She guessed that was only because she grew up as a girl alone in a world that thought of lone girls as little more than meat to be stolen at any opportunity. She had to be on her guard — she hadn't had a father to protect her since she was seven.

Eli helped, of course, but he was only a few months older than her; if someone decided they liked the looks of the little girl walking down the street, there wasn't much the little boy beside her could do.

Eli could call her paranoid all he wanted, but it was that paranoia that kept her alive for the last ten years.

Ember turned back toward the drift, ready now to believe that the blueness of the light that was so disturbing her was only a trick of her mind and not some indication that something was wrong around her. She could use a little more sleep, and night was falling — there was no point to continuing on now, not when they had decent shelter. But as she turned, something caught her eye. There was something large and spiky poking out from behind the drift.

Ember stepped around the hill of snow to take a better look and gasped. The cold air rushed into her, stabbing its way down into the center of her chest and momentarily freezing her entire airway. She buried her mouth down into the collar of her coat and sucked in air warmed by her own exhale.

But her eyes stayed fixed on the sight before her. The air shimmered faintly blue, reflecting the light that sparked off the walls and spires of the buildings that seemed to go on forever in either direction in front of her.

She didn't want to believe it, but there was nothing else she could make of the sight.

They'd done it. They found Frost.

Chapter Two

FOR A LONG MOMENT, Ember just stared, her thoughts struggling to grasp what her eyes were telling her.

It was real. It was here.

They'd found Frost.

She knew it had been a real place once. A thriving, vibrant city, the epicenter of culture and industry and art, nestled inside an endless forest. Ember knew this the way everybody in Dusk knew such things because stories of Before were a particular favorite pastime, a way to while away the endless winter nights.

But there was only one person left in Dusk who could even claim to remember Before, and old Korrah was probably mad with age by now. Ember knew Before existed, but only in the way a child who'd grown up in war knew the concept of peace. It was possible, sure, but dreaming of the possibility didn't help survive in reality.

Eli was the dreamer, the one who believed that the world could be different from the way it was. The one who sat at old Korrah's feet and listened with hope and desire brimming inside him for the things she said.

Ember wasn't a dreamer. Not really. Not like Eli. She'd come because … well, because. Because she couldn't help it. Because Eli needed her. Because if he died out here, there would truly be nothing left in all the world for her.

Because, deep down in that place that tugged at her, she knew she had to.

But she didn't actually expect to find anything but tundra and more tundra. The part of her she couldn't help might insist that there had to be something beyond Dusk, but the practical part of her knew there wasn't. At least nothing of meaning. Nothing they could *find*, at any rate. Eli's stories were just that: stories and nothing more. Frost wasn't real. Her compass wasn't actually pointing to something — it was just an old manufactured artifact that she couldn't figure out how to realign.

And yet…

Frost sat there, sparkling in the twilight not a hundred paces away from where they'd dug in to wait out the storm, like a mockery of all her most sensible thoughts.

Ember was finally able to detach her gaze from the sight long enough to crawl back into their little cave. Eli was still asleep in the bag; she shook his shoulder. He groaned and rolled over. "Few more minutes," he mumbled into his pack.

"Eli, get up. You'll want to see this."

He cracked open one eye. "See what?"

She couldn't hold back the smile. "Frost. Eli, we've found Frost!"

He sat up. His head brushed the top of their little hole, powdering him with crystalline specks of snow and ice. "What?"

Ember didn't wait for him to finish waking up or struggling to understand what she was saying. She just crawled back out of the hole, gesturing for him to follow. And a moment later, he'd slid into his boots and was scrambling out after her, one arm stuck through his coat and the other reaching blindly around his back for the other sleeve.

He stopped worrying about the coat when he got out of the drift and saw. His eyes, usually narrowed against the glare, grew wide, and his jaw came unhinged. "Mother Atalanta," he breathed.

His eyes scanned all the way to the left, then to the right — both directions were entirely taken up by the tall, blank-faced, blue-tinted wall that surrounded the spires behind it. He glanced at Ember long enough for a smile to start forming on his face, but then he went back to staring at the wall. His breaths puffed into the air like the beginnings of a laugh.

Ember cleared her throat and tried to shake away her own shock and awe long enough to figure out what they should do next. Her eyes caught on Eli's coat, dangling from one shoulder as he'd abandoned his attempts to get both arms inside it. She grabbed the dangling side and looped it around his shoulder so at least the sleeve cuff wasn't hitting the ground. "Don't tell me we've come all this way just to look at it," she said briskly.

Her words shook Eli out of his trance. He glanced down, seemed to notice that it was cold, and put his arm into his sleeve. "No. No, of course not. C'mon."

He took a step toward the wall; Ember whistled once, a short, sharp sound that broke through whatever thoughts were cluttering up his head, and he glanced back at her. She bobbed her head toward the snowdrift — and, more specifically, their packs and thermals and the bag still scattered around the shelter.

Eli grinned a bit sheepishly and turned back toward the drift.

Ember slithered back in and shoved their stuff out.

"We should wrap up. We don't know how long we'll be out here."

Eli didn't protest. They both wrapped themselves back up in their layers of knits and thermals. The darkness was coming in a hurry now, and the bluish light coming from the city was too dim to see by. Ember dug around in the front pocket of her pack, through the dried — and frozen — meat and extra knitted layers of clothing, until she found the small oil lamp and tin of oil she'd brought along for just this sort of thing. She filled the lamp and lit it with one of her five remaining matches, then put the tin and the four other matches back in the pack, burying them between layers of clothes in an attempt — so far successful — of keeping both dry. Then, shouldering her pack and holding up the lamp to light their way, she started toward the wall.

Walking was easier now that the wind and the weather had died down. Even though night was coming fast enough that Ember could actually see the light fading, the lamp flame was steady and bright enough to light their way.

They reached the wall in minutes. Eli went right up to it and touched it softly with one mittened hand, then let out another almost-laugh when that hand actually bumped against the solid wall. He tilted his head back and looked up at the wall, which went up to a dozen or more times his height and now obscured the buildings behind it from view. "I'm not dreaming," he whispered to himself.

"Do you need me to pinch you?" Ember whispered back.

He waved a silencing hand at her without looking over. She could almost hear the way his thoughts turned slightly sour towards her. How could she be so cavalier right now?

In truth, Ember was no less awed by the fact of this

wall, this city, than Eli was. But something was bothering her again. Like the bluish tint of the light that had made her unable to close her eyes back in the drift. Something was not quite right. She couldn't quite figure out what it was.

The wall in front of them was as smooth and clear as ice on still water, but when she got close to it, she realized she couldn't see through it. Everything behind the wall was concealed behind a clear blue tint that seemed to waver as Ember shifted the lamp from right hand to left. It was impossible to tell how thick the wall was, and there didn't appear to be any way through.

Eli seemed to be noticing the same things she had, only slightly belatedly. "How do we get in?"

"I don't know." Ember turned from side to side, shining the lamp as far in either direction as the light would go. "I don't see any door or archway or anything."

"Maybe on the other side?"

Ember frowned. The wall continued in either direction as far as she could see. There wasn't an "other side" they could get to. But she just nodded. "Maybe."

"C'mon. Let's go see what we can find." Eli turned left, probably at random, and started walking, leaving Ember to catch up.

They walked in silence. Ember was tempted to suggest that they stop for the night, but one glance at Eli's face told her that would be a losing proposition. "We're outside the walls of Frost, and you want to sleep?" she could imagine him saying.

But the farther they walked alongside the smooth wall without any way to get through it, the less hopeful Ember became. It would make sense, in its way, if the walls had no door. This was Frost, supposedly the last place in the world with light and warmth and industry. The only place in the world that had recovered, even a little, from the death of the Engine. If it had a door, surely it would be hounded continually by people trying to get in.

Dusk had a wall with doors, but there was nothing in Dusk worth protecting, and the wall had long ago fallen into disrepair. This wall was clearly not so ill cared for, which suggested to Ember that there were some things inside it worth the effort to protect. A door would be a weakness.

Ember was about to revisit her idea of suggesting they stop for the night, this time with the added force of the fact that they'd been walking for hours without finding a way into the city. And it had been hours. The lamp burned for six hours when it was full. She filled it before lighting it, and now it was three-quarters empty. She had just opened her mouth to break the silence and say she was tired, and they were wasting oil doing something they could just as easily do in daylight tomorrow when Eli suddenly bounded forward. Ember scanned ahead and saw what he saw: a break in the icy smoothness of the wall a hundred steps in front of them.

A door? Ember couldn't quite tell, but the target pushed her forward, making her jog behind Eli on legs so tired that her knees trembled with every step.

They reached the break and saw that yes, it was a door, but a door unlike anything Ember had ever seen. It was huge, as tall as the wall itself, and made like the wall out of clear, blue-tinted ice. Intricate designs were carved into the ice, stretching up its entire length. Arching across its top was a massive curve of ice. Ember thought she could see words carved into the arch, but when she stepped back and held up the lamp in an attempt to read them, her eyes caught instead on the shadowy figure of someone standing on the arch looking down at them.

Ember pulled down the scarf and thermal across her mouth. "H-hello?" she called up to the shape.

The figure didn't move. Didn't answer.

"Hello?" Her voice was a little stronger the second time, and she was sure now it was loud enough to be heard. "You up there!"

Eli stepped back and looked up. "What are you—" he began but was interrupted by a loud noise from the door itself.

The ice moved slowly, scraping harshly against the snow piled up against it, and from the center of the massive space, someone poked their head out. It was tiny against the backdrop of the gigantic doors: a woman with long, uncovered hair and bare shoulders.

Ember stared at her for a long moment. She'd never seen another person's uncovered shoulders. What could this woman be thinking, wearing such a thing outside and away from a roaring fire?

The woman stared back. Ember could see her eyes sweeping up and down the length of her body, then Eli's in turn. Finally, she called out to them, her voice barely tinted with something that might've been either exasperation or amusement. "Well, come on, then. You're letting in the cold!"

Chapter Three

EMBER AND ELI glanced at each other, Eli suddenly looking as uncertain as Ember felt. It didn't seem like the sort of greeting they, as mysterious strangers, should be receiving. It certainly wasn't the sort of greeting anyone approaching the walls of Dusk would receive.

Eli cleared his throat. "Should we...?"

"Well, we didn't come all this way just to look at it," Ember said.

His eyes crinkled at the corners with the smile hidden behind his scarf. "No, I guess not."

He took a step toward the woman and the doors, once again leaving Ember to follow.

The woman stepped aside and waved them through. "Quickly, now, if you please." She had a strange accent, thin and liquidy, one word barely ended before the next one began, as though they couldn't wait to be spoken. "We mustn't keep the doors open too long."

Ember slid through. She tried to ignore the flash of fear that rose up inside her as she hurried through the tunnel of ice that made up most of the trip through the door. As she scurried through, she realized just how thick the wall was.

That was why they weren't able to see through the clear bluish ice to the other side. Even the purest, clearest ice obscured vision when it was thick enough. It startled her to realize just how thick it was. She'd seen ice before — she'd never really known much else. But this much ice, so smooth and flawless, without any cracks or seams from building with ice bricks, was a marvel. It was like the entire wall had risen from a single gigantic sheet of pure water.

Was it magic or science? Ember didn't really believe in magic, but she'd heard the stories, same as everyone, of science so advanced that it might as well be magic.

Her father always told her that magic was science waiting to be understood.

And Ember wanted to understand. She'd been uncertain about this whole trip, but now that she was here, and she could see with her own eyes that it was all real, she wanted to understand it.

She made it through the tunnel in a few moments, and the woman hauled the door shut — apparently, it was as heavy as it looked. Inside the wall were the buildings of the city. The spires that had first caught Ember's eye were behind the rows of shorter buildings immediately before them.

Eli stepped toward the nearest building two paces away and put his hand on it. "Wood," he muttered, then turned to Ember with another smile lighting up his eyes. "They're made of wood!"

"Like from trees?"

He waved her forward, then grabbed her wrist and pressed her hand to the side of the building. "Do you feel that?"

She did, even through the thermal layer of her mitten.

18

The slight bumps as her fingers ran down the side of the building, the tiny snags in her mitten like miniature hooks grabbing at and releasing the fabric. She let out a breath like the ones Eli had made at the first sight of the wall, little noise that could've turned into an awed laugh if she allowed it.

She'd heard of wood and trees the same way she'd heard of warmth and industry, as memories turning to fantasy in the stories of Dusk's oldest residents. One of them had even had some wood: a spoon, split with cold and age, that she'd let Ember hold once. She couldn't imagine using such a thin thing to build with, but Korrah had sworn it was all true, that in the time Before, they'd built buildings not only with wood but with metal and rock and dirt.

The woman at the door cleared her throat softly. She smiled brightly, so brightly that the blue tint that curved up above their heads was reflected on her teeth. "Follow me, if you please. I'll show you to your apartments." She swept forward, down the street between the rows of wooden buildings, the hem of her dress swishing lightly against her knees.

Eli hurried after her. His gaze had moved from the buildings to the woman, and he stared at her with an expression that made Ember want to wrinkle her nose in disgust and then tease him about it so he would be embarrassed and stop staring at her.

Though Ember couldn't deny that the woman was worth staring at, she was just as novel as the wooden buildings and the flawless ice wall. The way she was dressed was absurd. It took a few minutes of following her for Ember to notice that she was growing too warm inside her thermals, that the temperature of the air around them had changed. She began to remove her layers, stripping off goggles and scarf and hood as they walked, and found that there was actual warmth inside the walls.

Even still, the woman's dress was absurd. Yes, there was warmth in the air, but it was chilly enough to keep the wall of ice and the buildings well frozen. Ice melted to water at a temperature that even people in Dusk considered cool enough to warrant long sleeves and long leggings — not that Dusk ever got warm enough to melt ice — so what was this woman doing walking around in a thin dress that covered neither her shoulders nor anything past her knees? Couldn't she feel the chill in the air just as much as Ember's newly bared hands and face did? And yet, she walked along just a step ahead of them with bare legs and even barer arms, making Eli ogle like the stupid boy he still was.

They turned down a new street. As they went deeper into the city, away from the wall, the squat wooden buildings were replaced with taller, spikier ice buildings. The air was warming more as well, and soon Ember was sweating beneath her shirt. This worried her: sweat turned to ice, and that could drop a person's core temperature almost before they knew what was happening. She tried to remove more layers as she could — first the outermost thermal ones, then unwrapping the next inner knitted layers. But the air continued to warm, somehow not melting the buildings around them.

Magic or science?

Finally, the woman paused at the bottom of one of the tall ice buildings and turned her too-wide smile back at them. "This way, if you please." She opened the door to the building and waved them in ahead of her.

It was only as she stepped through the door that Ember realized the building wasn't made of ice: it was made of glass.

She wasn't sure if this was true about all the other buildings they'd passed, but she saw it now clear as could be. Huge panes of thick, transparent glass that offered the building as clear a view to the street outside as if they weren't standing inside a building.

Glass, like wood, was one of those items that Ember knew about and had even seen bits of, had heard stories about people using it to build with, but had never actually thought those stories were really real. In Dusk, you made your shelters of snow and ice. More permanent places, ones made Before, were made of animal skins and furs, with bone or ice supports to keep the skins from collapsing. But no new places made with such materials were possible because animals had been gone for as long as Ember could remember — all frozen or starved to death. What they had was all they would ever have.

But that wasn't so here. She'd barely stepped into the building when she was struck again by how different the people of Frost lived. The air in the building was warm — not just not cold like it was outside, but actually warm, though she couldn't see any evidence of a fire pit. The floor was thick with furs and rugs, so numerous that they practically overlapped.

The woman shut the glass door behind them and marched on ahead. Her choice of clothing made a bit more sense now. She paused when she noticed that neither Ember nor Eli were following her this time and returned to them, still lingering just inside the door.

The woman smiled broadly — that seemed to be the only expression she had. "It's all right," she said. "We have apartments prepared for you upstairs."

Upstairs? And *prepared* for them? Ember shot Eli a worried glance and saw, for the first time, a similar hint of worry reflected back in his eyes. He was the first to turn away, to look back at the woman. "Were you..." He licked his lips. "Were you expecting us?"

The woman's smile somehow, impossibly, got wider. She had large, square teeth that glared almost as brightly as snow in sunlight. "We have apartments prepared for all our visitors. Follow me."

Which was not an answer to the question, but Eli nodded as though it was and followed the woman. Ember hesitated, torn. The initial awe was starting to wear off. She felt suddenly suspicious of this oddly friendly woman with her bare shoulders and bright smile. And the fact that she hadn't given a proper answer to Eli's perfectly straight-forward yes-or-no question turned that vague feeling of something-wasn't-right into active suspicion. Because, if she was actually as friendly and accommodating as she wanted to appear, why not just say yes, someone had seen them as they walked for hours along the length of the wall, or no, they were being taken to apartments that were held in a state of readiness for anyone who might come by. Either one would've made perfect sense to Ember and would've answered the question without being suspicious.

Only people with something to hide dodged questions with shifty answers.

And yet, Eli followed her as though his own suspicions had been alleviated by the woman's non-answer. He glanced back at her now, grinning, and waved her after them.

Ember let out a breath. It seemed that her primary goal of keeping Eli safe and out of trouble hadn't yet been achieved.

The woman led them to a large staircase at the back of the room. It was made of metal spiraling up around a thick central pole and then disappearing into the thick glass ceil-ing. The rail on the outside of the spiral was smooth, as though worn by thousands of hands, and each of the evenly spaced spokes that held the railing attached to the stairs were actually hundreds of tiny black filaments, each barely thicker than a hair, woven together in a massive, intricate braid. Two steps above her, Eli had his eyes fixed on those braided struts. His jaw was hanging loose in wonder.

Ember clenched her own jaw as tight as it would go and followed up the stairs.

At the top, they found a long hallway carpeted with furs and lined with doors. Glass had been replaced by wood here, painted the same kind of bright white as the snow. The woman led them a short way down the hall, then gestured to one of the doors. "Here we are." She backed away a few steps, back toward the staircase. "If you need anything, you can ask for Maudie."

Eli smiled back. "Is that you? Maudie?"

"Thanks be to the queen," the woman answered and turned that overly bright smile onto him.

Ember cleared her throat. "Thank you."

The woman smiled. "Thanks be to the queen," she said like she was correcting her.

Eli set his hand on the knob and nudged open the door. "C'mon, Ember. I'm ready to get some sleep."

She nodded, but her eyes stayed on Maudie and that unnaturally bright smile until Eli opened the door, put a hand on her shoulder, and drew her inside the room after him.

The door slammed shut behind her, and Ember thought she heard the click of a lock against the frame.

Chapter Four

EMBER SPUN TOWARD THE DOOR, her heart thundering in her ears.

"What?" Eli asked, startled.

"Did you hear that? She locked us in!"

Eli turned to the door, too. He dropped his hand to the doorknob and gave it an experimental turn. The knob turned without resistance, and the door popped open a finger's width. He pushed it the rest of the way and glanced out into the hall. Maudie was gone.

Ember's heart stopped throbbing, but the rush of adrenaline that had come with her spike of panic lingered, zipping down her arms and making her veins feel like they were being frozen into threads of ice.

Eli chuckled and closed the door again. The latch clicked into place. "Is that what you heard?"

Ember frowned but had to concede the possibility. "Maybe."

He shook his head and looked around the room. Like the place downstairs, it was large and open and warm despite the obvious lack of fire, the floor layered with rugs of fur so thick their boots made visible indentations. The wall farthest from the door was all glass and looked out over several other buildings on the road they'd been walking down before turning inside. Sitting just inside the glass wall was a large couch and, in front of the couch, a low wooden table. On the center of the table was a tray made of silver metal buffed to a mirror shine and holding a bright white teapot and two small white teacups.

Eli flopped into the couch, letting out a low groan of pleasure and relief as he got off his feet. After a moment, he opened his eyes and smiled over at Ember, who still hadn't moved from her spot just inside the door. "Come. Sit. It's really comfortable."

Ember walked over to the couch and lowered herself gingerly into one of the cushions. It was thick and soft, begging for her to flop back into it like Eli had done, but she didn't dare sit back.

She wasn't sure why. Her body ached with exhaustion, and her muscles trembled with the desire to relax. She wanted to sit back and soak in the warmth of the room, not centralized at a small oil fire but diffuse and everywhere, like the cold she was used to. But she couldn't sit back. If she did, if she settled into the warm, soft embrace of the cushions, there was no telling when she would be able to get back up again.

Eli sat up and reached for the teapot. He poured something thick and brown and steaming into the cup, then lifted the cup to his lips.

"Don't!" Ember protested. "You don't know what that is!"

He lifted an eyebrow at her in the expression she hated the most, the one that said she was being paranoid again

— and that stubbornly ignored the fact that she was just trying to look out for him. "You think Maudie brought us into the city and all the way to this nice and unlocked room just to poison us?"

"I don't know what I think," Ember shot back, more harshly than she meant to speak to him. "But this place." She hesitated, glanced around. "It's weird."

"It's *different*," he said, stressing the word as though him saying it with deliberate firmness would change the way Ember felt.

"It's *weird*," she said back in the same tone. "Did you see how she was dressed? Like a picture of a woman from Before. Like the world isn't all ice and snow and cold everywhere."

Eli snorted. "Is that what has you so worked up? Seeing a woman's ankles?"

She flushed but lifted her chin and answered between tight lips. "If I'm worked up, it's because you don't seem to be taking this seriously."

"Taking it … Ember, we did it. We found Frost!" He took a sip from the teacup. His eyes closed, and he groaned again. "You have to try this." He opened his eyes and held out the teacup.

She took it and peered into it warily. The liquid inside was so thick that it left a trail up over the rim of the cup where Eli had sipped it. It steamed gently, and the steam smelled sweet and rich.

"Go on," he urged. "You'll like it."

She looked over at him for a long moment, waiting to see if he would fall over poisoned and trying to decide what she could do if he did. The hallway appeared empty — not that it was necessarily so, but she doubted there was anyone near enough to hear her scream for help. But Eli just looked straight back at her, his lips starting to tip up into a mocking little grin until he finally broke the silence. "I feel fine," he said like he was answering a question.

"I didn't ask you how you felt."

"You wanted to."

"No."

"It's not poisoned."

"I never said it was."

"Try it. It's good. I don't know what it is — not broth or tea — but you'll like it."

He wasn't going to let it go, not until she took a sip. So she did, at least as much to prove to him that she didn't think it was poisoned as because she was curious.

It was good. Thick and sweet, just hot enough to sting the inside of her mouth and soak through her throat and stomach when she swallowed. She'd never tasted anything like it or anything close enough like it to even begin to understand what it was. A noise escaped her throat, a sound of pleasure that didn't wait for her permission to be uttered.

And, even as the flavor lingered, she didn't feel poisoned.

"Told you."

Ember opened her eyes. She didn't recall shutting them. "I wasn't arguing with you."

He grabbed the pot again and filled the second cup, then sat back and sipped at his own drink. His eyes kept moving around the room like he was expecting any moment to be awakened from the dream, and he wanted to hold onto this place for as long as he could. "We did it," he muttered, apparently more to the teacup in his hand than to Ember beside him. "We found Frost."

"Yeah." Ember set the cup back on the tray. She

wanted another sip but couldn't help feel that one was already too much. "Now what?"

He frowned at her.

"What?"

"Can't you just relax? Just for a minute? You're making me anxious sitting like that."

"Like what?"

"Like you keep expecting someone to break down the door. We're in Frost, Ember! The last great city in the world. It's not imaginary. They have buildings made of wood and glass and rugs made of fur and drinks made of … whatever this is. If you aren't excited to be here, why did you even come?"

Ember sat up a little straighter. "Because you begged me until I said yes."

"That's a lie, and we both know it."

"Because you would've died out there on your own."

He took another sip of the drink. There was something profoundly insufferable about the way he was not quite grinning over it. "Try again."

"Because…" A dozen other reasons crowded into her head. Because he wasn't the only one who longed to believe there was more than just ice and snow and cold in the world. Because there would be nothing left for her in Dusk if Eli left.

But she couldn't say those things; they smacked too close to the truth.

"Because it's none of your business."

He grinned. "I know why. It's because you were curious, too. You wanted to know if the stories were true. But you don't want to admit it to yourself because that would mean you've been taken in by old Korrah's mad stories."

"She isn't mad."

"Clearly. She's old. She remembers things. Things from

Before. This!" He gestured expansively around the room with the hand not holding the teacup. "This is what the world could be. We don't have to sit around in the cold and dark, pretending that our rations won't run out before we do. We can have hope now."

Ember scowled. "You're not a storybook hero, Eli. You won't be able to bring the world back to the way it was before just because you survived a trip through a blizzard."

She knew she was hitting him in the place it would most hurt, that tender part in the center of all his dreaming, but she couldn't stop herself. Finding Frost wasn't going to solve the world's problems or save Dusk from its inevitable slow, frozen, starving death.

Eli went quiet, his jaw tightening. Ember did feel bad about saying things so bluntly — he didn't deserve her attitude or suspicions. The fact that he got them anyway was just an unfortunate byproduct of the fact that he'd been the only other person she could talk to for the last several days, and really most of her life. She knew what she said was true, but she wished she didn't have to say it.

"Sorry," she muttered, her eyes falling to her hands.

They were quiet for a while. Ember fiddled with the cuffs of her long shirt sleeves, tugging them down over her hands and pushing them back up, mostly because it gave her bare, too-warm fingers something to do.

Finally, Eli set down his teacup and looked at her. "I'm not trying to change the whole world. I know I can't. But I was hoping to save our lives. There was nothing for us back there. You knew that. You saw it. That's why I needed you to come with me. And that's why you came."

Ember let out a breath, and slowly, so slowly that the motion actually hurt, she leaned back into the couch. "You're right. That's why I came."

"And we did it," he whispered. "We made it."

"We did." She glanced over at him and smiled just a little. "And now what do we do?"

He smiled back, just as small but with absolute sincerity. "Whatever we want. We make our own lives now."

Chapter Five

A KNOCK on the door startled Ember awake. She didn't remember falling asleep on the couch, or even at what point she'd closed her eyes and let her head fall against Eli's shoulder. But obviously, she had, and now she groaned as she sat back up, blinking hard to try and make her surroundings come back into focus. Couch. Low wooden table with a teapot and two cups coated with a layer of the thick brown beverage inside the pot. Eli was on the couch, too, his head tilted sideways, so it had until a moment ago rested on the top of hers.

The sense of a voice pulling at her, begging for help, was just a dream. It flickered away in the sudden reality of the room.

Another knock. Eli got to his feet, stretching, and went to the door. The woman, Maudie, stood on the other side, already smiling her white-out bright smile.

"I must apologize for neglecting you," she said. Her voice sounded thin and strained, though Ember couldn't tell if that was because of the smile that stretched her lips as tight as a drum over her teeth. "It's rare for Frost to receive visitors."

She stopped as though waiting for an answer, but Ember didn't know what to say.

Eli shook his head, dismissing the woman's apology. "It's fine. I think we both just fell asleep."

"You must've come a very long way."

Ember stood. Her muscles all ached, but she didn't want to shake them out in front of the woman and reveal any kind of weakness. She didn't join Eli in front of the door but hung back, watching and waiting.

For what, she wasn't sure, but she felt she would definitely know it when it happened.

There was a beat of silence, a moment stretched just a little too thin. Eli cleared his throat. "Do you need to come in?"

"If you please."

"Sure. Um … come in." He stepped back and held open the door.

Maudie went straight for the couch and sat herself down. She was holding a thin board with several sheets of paper clipped to it. She flipped through the papers, though Ember suspected that gesture was an affect since she didn't seem to see anything in them, and immediately turned her attention back to her and Eli. "As I said, we don't often have visitors in Frost, so protocols have become somewhat confused. I must apologize for this and will see to it myself that it will not happen again."

"It's really fine." Eli came away from the door and set himself half a step forward of where Ember still stood, as though he was preparing to take the brunt of whatever this Maudie woman was about to throw at them.

He could say what he wanted about how there was no need for any of Ember's instinctive suspicion, but it was clear to her that he felt something odd about this, too, or he wouldn't've snapped into protective-big-brother mode quite so fast.

"There are a few details to handle in order to settle you in properly, so I was sent to handle them." Another shuffle of papers, though this time Maudie's attention actually focused on them, and she seemed to consider something on them. "You have an appointment tomorrow at sunrise to pay your tribute to our queen. Until then, you are free to move about as you please. Here are your tokens for the day." She reached into a pocket sewn to the breast of her dress and pulled out a small bag that jingled as she set it down on the table in front of her. "You will be given a per-diem salary of ten rubuls apiece. If you wish to contest that, you may file a complaint with the treasury, though" — she leaned forward, her voice dropping as though sharing a secret — "you ought not to expect your complaint to be addressed for six to eight weeks. It is the treasury, you know."

She paused like she expected them to laugh and nod and agree with her. *Oh, sure, we know all about the treasury.* Eli shifted his weight uncomfortably from one foot to the other; Ember crossed her arms over her chest and frowned.

Maudie cleared her throat and replastered her smile, which had begun to slip just a notch, back onto her face. Ember couldn't help but wonder if the woman's cheeks ever got sore. "After you've spoken with the queen, I imagine there will be work found for you. Do you have any special interests or talents that could be used in service of our queen?"

There was another pause, longer than the awkward silence from when she first came in. Eli glanced at Ember, who didn't dare take her eyes off of Maudie in case the woman was still trying to get up to something.

It was the smile, she'd decided. Not just that it was too big and overly bright, but that Maudie seemed determined to hold onto it even when the moment didn't actually call for it. Her eyes stayed so empty, with only the smile stretching her lips so thin that Ember wondered how they didn't crack and split apart under the strain. It wasn't natural.

"I don't know," Eli answered.

"Think hard. Surely there is something."

"Well, Ember's good with machines."

Maudie's smile turned to her. Ember glared at Eli, who shrugged helplessly. "You're good with machines?"

"I-I don't know." Ember didn't mean to stutter and could've kicked herself for doing it. "I tinker sometimes."

"She's being modest," Eli cut in. "She's been building things since she could bash two stones together. Remember Korrah's clock? That mechanical plow you got running again? Even your compass — you've been tinkering with that for years."

Maudie's smile remained unflappable, though her voice, dropping into a whisper, sounded like a frown. "Are you a *scientist?*"

Ember laughed, one hard single-syllable noise escaping the grip she'd been keeping on her feelings. But that word — scientist — tangled up in her already-snarled thoughts and threatened to drag along with it thoughts and memories she didn't want to deal with, especially not in front of this strange Frost woman. "Oh, no, nothing so formal as that. I'm a tinkerer at best."

Maudie looked back down at her papers, and this time, she pulled out an ink pen and made some marks on the topmost one. Then she looked up again and beamed. "I'll be back tomorrow to take you to the queen."

She slid out of the room and closed the door softly behind her.

Eli was already investigating the contents of the bag when Ember, sure that Maudie had left, turned away from the door. He tipped the little drawstring-closed bag over his palm, and several small copper-colored coins spilled out from it.

Eli's eyes widened, and Ember could feel her own doing the same even as she fought against the sudden flush of wonder those coins inspired. She peered at them, a little uncertainly. "Money?"

"I think so." He tipped his hand this way and that, watching the coins as they sparkled dimly in the faint sunlight coming through the window-wall behind the couch.

Ember had never seen money before. She'd seen coins — she used to play with her father's handful of coins when she was little, lining them up in various arrangements or putting them into a little bag and shaking them around to make noise — but money was a thing of the past, a relic of Before.

"This place is weird." She was pretty sure that she'd said that, those exact words, before. "How can they just *give* money to strangers?"

Maybe the money had no value. It was the most sensible option.

Eli poured the coins back into the bag. "Maybe they have enough. They can afford to be generous."

"You think it's generosity?"

"There's been no reason to think otherwise. Maudie's been nothing but friendly."

"She doesn't worry you?"

"No."

"But that smile? It's so … unnatural."

"She's friendly." He let out a breath. "Why are you always so quick to assume the worst in people? Not everyone is out to take advantage of you. And this is Frost. They can afford it."

"I'm not arguing with you about this again."

"Good. Because I don't want to, either." He walked over to the other side of the room, pushing open a door they hadn't looked through when they came into the room. "Oooh," he whispered, more like a sigh than a word, then glanced over his shoulder and smiled. "I found the beds."

"I'm going to go for a walk. See what I can find out."

She wondered if she'd be allowed to leave the building, if Maudie or a guard or someone would try to stop her. Surely there were guards around. Surely there was someone watching to make sure they weren't here to steal or make trouble in the city.

"Okay," Eli answered. His attention was back on the room that apparently held the beds. He stepped inside.

Ember followed, disconcerted by his lack of concern. It had become something of a theme with him these last few days. The other room did have beds; three of them, in fact, spaced evenly along the back wall of the room. To the right, the glass wall from the main room continued, and Ember wondered if there was anywhere in this apartment that wasn't potentially visible from the outside.

That's how she would keep an eye on them, she decided. By watching them through the glass walls.

Eli flopped onto the bed nearest the glass and snuggled himself down under a thick, bright white blanket. He'd kicked off his boots at some point while they'd been on the couch, and she could see the small mound in the blanket that must've been made by his toes, wriggling like he was rolling his ankles beneath the blanket. His head sunk into the thick white pillows at the head of the bed, so far that it practically disappeared. He closed his eyes and smiled blissfully at nothing.

"So. I'm going to leave now."

"Don't get lost."

Ember scoffed. She knew how to make her way around a place.

She sensed that he was mostly calling her bluff, but now that she'd made the bluff, she was curious. Would they let her leave? Was she free to walk out of this room, down the spiral staircase, and out into the open streets?

Eli cracked open one eye. "You still here?"

Ember straightened. "If I'm not back by sunset, then you can assume I've been harvested for meat."

The eye closed. "Will do."

She lingered another moment, waiting for him to say something else, but he only rolled onto his side, his breaths already steadying into the rhythm of sleep.

She turned away, grabbed the little bag of coins, and emptied it into her pant pockets where they should be safe beneath the hem of her shirt. She grabbed the bulky knitted sweater from where she'd left it on the floor near the couch, leaving the thermals because she recalled on coming into the city that she'd begun to sweat with the thermals on — she hadn't bothered yet to take off her boots — then went to the door and tried the handle.

She still expected it to resist her, despite the fact that it had been unlocked every time she'd seen it tried. But no, just as it had the other times, the knob turned without resistance, the door opened, and Ember stepped out into the hallway.

Chapter Six

SHE WALKED down the hall with light steps, doing her best to minimize the thud of her heavy boots on the rug-lined floor. She passed several doors in the hallway, and all seemed silent behind each one.

No one met her in the hall.

She went down the stairs. Her boots thudded much louder on the metal stairs than they had across the rugs, but again, no one seemed to be around to hear her and wonder why the stranger was clomping down the steps.

The ground floor of the building was as quiet and empty as the upper floor had seemed to be. Ember felt her skin prickling. This was supposed to be a great city — from what she was able to see out of the building's glass sides, it *was* a great city, the greatest in all that was left of the world. So why was this building, and indeed this entire street, so empty? She pictured Dusk on the rare occasion that the sun came out; it became a hub of noise and activity, people trying to soak up what little light and warmth they could hope for and taking advantage of that light and warmth to air out clothes and tidy homes as best they could.

But the street outside the building appeared as quiet and empty as the building itself. Ember set her fingers on the handle of the room's glass door and steeled herself for this one to be locked, for her to have finally found the catch in all this supposed hospitality. But the door swung inward when she pulled, and a light breeze, colder than the air inside the building but warmer than any breeze she'd ever known, swirled through the open door as if the air itself was trying to prove her suspicions unfounded.

"Alright," she said, out loud in case the guards that ought to be watching her were merely hiding out of her sight. "I'm leaving now." She set one foot firmly across the threshold and outside of the building.

No one jumped out from some hiding place to stop her and haul her back to the room upstairs. The building and the street remained still and quiet.

She brought her other foot out of the building. The door closed behind her with a soft hiss like a near-silent exhalation.

Ember walked away from the building, her eyes continuously scanning the space around her, still waiting for someone to tell her to stop, that she couldn't leave the apartment or be out in the streets. Every moment that nothing happened, she felt her anxiety rising.

It couldn't be this simple. She couldn't possibly be allowed to wander the streets. She was a stranger, an outsider, and Frost was the most glorious city in the world — there was no way someone wasn't watching her.

But nothing hindered her as she continued to step away from the building and out into the quiet streets.

As she stepped out of the shadow of the building, she

felt the sun hit her full on her exposed face and hands. She held out one hand, turned the palm up toward the sun, and tried to soak in the feeling. The light seemed to shimmer faintly blue on the rough skin of her palm; when she glanced up in the direction of the sun, she could see the whole sky shimmering in just that same way, with the same faintly blue sheen that had first attracted her attention to the place.

A force field. Ember had never seen one, but she'd read about them in the books her father had cherished. She stared up at the sky for a while, marveling.

That must be how the streets of Frost stayed clear and warm. She tried to remember what she knew about force fields: they were a lot like thermals, but for the air, trapping and reflecting heat that was generated from inside them, and they took some very large and sophisticated machines to create and maintain. Machines that could've only been made Before. Machines that were modeled on the great Engine itself and that only a handful of select scientists had ever even begun to understand.

Ember followed the arc of the force field as far in every direction as she could see it. As best she could tell, it seemed to cover the entirety of the city. She gaped, struggling to imagine the size and power of the machines that must keep up such a large field.

What she wouldn't give to see such machines, to look at them and try to understand how they worked.

Eventually, unable to tell where the force field began or ended, and her neck and eyes aching from the strain of looking up and trying to see something that kept shimmering out of sight the moment she thought she actually could see the field, she started onward down the street.

The streets here were laid out in neat squares. She'd noticed it earlier. The street she was on ran approximately parallel to the wall she and Eli had first seen. There were other equally straight-looking streets that intersected at regular intervals with the one she was on, and the intersections made what looked to her like perfect ninety-degree angles to each other.

After two blocks, she paused and let out a breath. So far, no one seemed to care that she was out of her room.

It didn't look like anyone was following her.

Ember scanned the intersection so she'd be able to recognize it again when she came back. The buildings all looked remarkably similar, tall with the outside as smooth as the ice — maybe it was glass? — wall they'd come through. Sunlight sparkled blindingly off of the buildings, making Ember's unprotected eyes water when she looked at them for too long. The streets were quiet, empty of people. But at the northeastern corner of the intersection, there was a building with a worn wooden sign hanging over its glass door. The sign was painted black, and in golden script letters, it said "Queen's Cross Cafe."

Ember pulled in and let out a breath. That seemed unique and memorable enough that she would recognize it again when she saw it. She tugged the hem of her sweater down over the opening of the pocket to limit the chances that someone would snatch her rubuls and turned left down the street that she hoped would take her away from the edge of the city.

People began appearing three blocks later, and though their presence heightened Ember's attention to what was happening around her, it also eased the anxiety she'd felt as she was forced to wonder if Frost was empty or abandoned. But, no. There were people here. Lots of them — though why she'd had to go so far to find them was a question she stashed away to puzzle at later. They were all dressed as impractically as Maudie. The women wore light sleeveless dresses that barely covered their knees and wide-brimmed hats without any ear protection. The men were a little less ridiculously dressed — at least their pants went down to their ankles, though most of them still had bared shoulders and the same sorts of wide-brimmed hats that couldn't possibly keep their heads warm. But none of them seemed to much notice or care that they were dressed like there was no chance of them losing their limbs to the cold; they strolled down the streets, talking and laughing, or hurried from one intersection to the next. Some came in and out of the buildings along the sides of the street, clutching bags made of paper and cloth to their chests.

Ember walked, joining in the general direction of the crowd. She kept expecting to hear someone point her out, demand to know what a stranger was doing in their midst, maybe even to grab her and stick a knife in her belly to harvest her meat — not that she'd be good pickings, especially compared to most of the people around her, but it was something she was so used to watching out for that she would probably never be able to turn it off no matter what happened or where she lived.

There wasn't a lot of cannibalism in Dusk, but it happened often enough to keep everyone wary of strangers in a crowd.

But no one seemed to give her more than a quick second glance. She saw heads turn toward her on occasion, maybe once with every few dozen people she passed, but when she met those people's eyes, they only smiled wide and nodded at her like she was an old acquaintance they couldn't quite recognize, then turned away and kept doing whatever they had been doing before.

Ember wasn't sure what to make of this reaction. On the one hand, it seemed friendly and innocuous, not worth the way it caused her heart to thunder in her ears and her fingers to curl into ready fists each time; on the other, it was too strange for her to ignore.

Why was everyone in Frost so eager to let her go about whatever she was doing? Why was no one more suspicious of her?

Why was no one watching her?

She tried to shake off the worry that was morphing into paranoia inside her. Maybe Eli was right, and people in Frost were so used to being comfortable that they could afford trust and generosity.

But that thought only irked her more. She wasn't ready to concede the point to Eli and his foolish lack of suspicion.

There was something going on inside this city, something that made Ember's skin prickle every time another person looked at her and smiled as wide as Maudie. It wasn't natural for people to be so accepting, so unconcerned, about a stranger in their midst — especially since, according to Maudie, Frost rarely had any visitors.

The flow of the crowd pulled her down a few more streets, all of them packed with buildings and people moving in and out of those buildings. Food smells began to catch her attention after another block: warm meats and drinks, spicy, savory scents that she had no words for. Inside the glass walls of one large, squat building, she saw rows and rows of food of all different colors, shapes, and sizes. People moved through the rows, ran their fingers across the slatted wooden boxes that held the food, picked up the individual items and squeezed or sniffed them, then dropped them into large bags or set them back in the boxes they'd come from.

Ember's mouth watered, but she didn't dare go into the place for the fear — probably exaggerated, but still plenty real — that leaving the crowd on the streets would be all the invitation someone would need to sneak up behind her to rob or kill her. While she was in the crowd, though she could feel along every inch of her from hat to boots how she stood out, there were enough people around that she could disappear if she needed to. Separating herself from the main crowd on the streets would make her stand out that much more.

So she let the motion of the people around her pull her away from the sight of all that food, pass another intersection, and deposit her into a space where the buildings pushed back, and the street opened up into a large rectangular space defined on three sides by the buildings and on the fourth and far side by a massive palace that seemed to be made almost entirely of tall, thin spires of clear bluish ice.

Ember's footsteps flagged and paused as she found herself facing the palace. It was so large and so near that she couldn't take it all in at once; she had to turn her head left, right, and up to see it completely. Some of the spires reached so high that they almost became obscured by the wavering bluish gleam of the force field.

The general flow of the crowd broke up as it spilled into the space. Many people continued straight forward, toward the palace and what Ember guessed were the front doors of the building, but many people also split off to go to the other buildings or to where there was a great sculpture sparkling in the dimming sunlight.

Ember wandered over to the sculpture, though her eyes remained mostly on the palace. Still, she was able to see the sculpture all at once, and that comforted her. It was a woman dressed in a dress similar in shape and cut to those worn by the women in the city. She held a long, thin spear raised in one hand, and curled at her feet was some kind of great monster, a beast with a thick body and tusks that curled from its mouth to almost the back of its head. On the base of the sculpture were words dug into the glass and worn almost completely away by the gentle swipes of the fingers of passersby. Ember could only just make out the words clearly enough to read. "Our mother Atalanta, hero, and explorer. May she forever keep us safe from the monsters Beyond."

It seemed a strange place for an altar to Atalanta. Still, the statue, clear bluish glass, with the spear lifted in triumph over her head and the dead beast at her feet, cut an imposing figure in front of the palace.

"This is nothing," said a male voice from just behind Ember's right shoulder. "You should see it in the moonlight."

Chapter Seven

EMBER YELPED and spun around to face the attacker. One of her hands went around his throat even as the other scrambled for the knife she usually carried tucked into the waistband of her pants. But her groping hand found only air and her thick knit sweater, and she remembered in another flash of near-panic that she'd taken the knife out when she'd shed her layers in the apartment.

How could she have been so stupid to step out of the room without her knife? She was in a strange city where she knew nothing and no one. If this stranger robbed her or dragged her into an alley to cut her up for meat, she might almost deserve it for being so unprepared to defend herself.

"Whoa, easy!" The other person lurched back, apparently surprised by the way she rounded on him. His hands came up in front of him, palms out and fingers splayed to prove he wasn't carrying a weapon. "I'm sorry. I didn't mean to startle you."

Ember narrowed her eyes. "Who are you? Why were you following me?"

His hair was orange, a surprising pop of color in the white and faintly blue space around her. She'd never seen hair that color before.

"Not following," he said, swallowing hard around the fingers at his throat. She wasn't squeezing, but it was clear by the shock in his face he understood that she could. "I just got here myself. From Fourth Street."

He said the name with significance, as though he expected her to recognize it. As though it proved he wasn't following her.

As the initial burst of panic eased, Ember began to see more of him. He was about her age, maybe just older, taller than her by a head, and dressed like the dozens of other Frost men in the square, though without the hat. A strap of a small cloth bag was slung over one shoulder, and the bag itself was half full of some of those brightly colored, roundish foods. His accent was like Maudie's: fast and liquid sounds eager to escape before their predecessors had been fully formed.

But it was the color of his hair that kept pulling at her attention. Like tongues of fire curling over his ears and spilling across his forehead. She wondered, fleetingly, pointlessly, if it would be hot to the touch.

Ember flicked her head to knock away such a thought and dropped her hand from his throat, suddenly aware of the other people in the square, a couple of whom standing at the other side of the Atalanta statue were openly staring at the commotion.

She wished she had her knife, but already her thoughts had switched to the ways she could incapacitate someone without it, at least for long enough to get a solid head start back into the safety of the crowd. A fist to the nose, an elbow to the stomach, a knee to the groin. She was smaller than him, but he was clearly much softer than her. If it came to a fight, it was a fight Ember was pretty sure she could win.

"It's okay," he said. His hands were still up in that I'm-not-armed position even as she let go of him. His voice took on a soothing tone, the sort a parent might use on a child who'd just screamed themselves awake with nightmares. "I'm sorry. I didn't mean to scare you."

Ember frowned, not sure if he was telling the truth. "Did Maudie send you?"

"No. There was no sending, no following. I live a few blocks away." He lowered his hands only slowly. A smile tugged at one corner of his lips. "I was out shopping."

Ember let out a breath and felt the tension in her shoulders ease just a little. "You shouldn't sneak up on people like that."

His lips twitched upward again. "Most people don't react quite so violently to someone trying to say hello."

"Is that what you were doing?"

Another twitch. After looking at the unnaturally bright smiles of the strangers around her, Ember found this boy's attempt to still his own smile oddly genuine. "Yes."

She huffed. "Well, you went about it all wrong."

"Noted. I'll be more considerate next time."

They were quiet for a moment. The boy lifted one hand and ran it through those fire-orange curls. "Name's Felix."

Another silence. He looked at her like he was expecting something.

"What?"

"And you are…?"

"Is this an interrogation?"

"It's called an introduction. Do they not have those in the outworld?"

"Outworld?" Ember repeated, uncertain.

He waved a hand in a vague gesture she assumed was meant to indicate everywhere outside of Frost. "Beyond the walls."

She didn't realize how much she'd relaxed until all the suspicions came flooding back. "How did you—"

He interrupted her with a soft, surprised laugh. "You don't hide it well."

She glanced down at her sweater, pants, and boots. And, probably even more than that, his shock at her reaction to being approached from behind made her wonder if the people of Frost were just used to strangers innocently coming up to them and talking, just to say hello. "Oh. Right."

"I told you my name. It seems only fair that you tell me yours."

Her gaze returned to him. There was something warm and genuine in his expression, not like Maudie, who was clearly putting on a show. The cold knot at the center of her stomach loosened. "Ember."

The boy — Felix — laid a palm flat against his chest and dipped his head. When his head came back up, he was smiling, though without the face-splitting wideness of other's smiles. It was just a nice smile. Normal and warm. "I'm sorry again for scaring you."

A smile of her own flickered across her face. "Me, too."

There was another, slightly longer, pause. Felix dropped his hand from his chest and used it to adjust the bag slung across his shoulder. "So. Is this your first time here in Frost?"

Ember nodded. "My friend and I got here — mmm …" She squinted up at the sky, trying to string together all the moments she'd been inside the city and decide how long it had already been. The sun was sinking quickly toward the horizon; apparently, Frost's days weren't much longer than Dusk's this time of year. "Last night, I think?"

"Your friend?" Felix repeated, glancing around the square.

"He's still back at the apartment. Sleeping. It's been a long trip."

There was a small change in Felix's expression, a subtle brightening of his eyes and a straightening of his spine. "Where are you from?"

A new suspicion prickled at Ember's skin. Why should a random Frost boy care where she was from, or what she was doing here, or anything at all about her?

The irony of her feelings wasn't lost on her. Ten minutes ago, she was suspicious because no one seemed to care who she was or where she was from; now, she was suspicious because someone did.

"Never mind. You don't have to tell me." Felix glanced around the square as though hoping to find his next words sitting at Atalanta's feet. One hand fluttered, uncertain, against his bag, and he smiled suddenly and reached inside. "Are you hungry?"

Could he hear the way her stomach was complaining? She hadn't had anything in it besides a mouthful of that thick brown drink since she'd left home.

Felix pulled out one of the colorful foodstuffs that weighed down his bag and held it out to her. It was bright red and sort of round, about the size of her two fists, pressed together.

She stared at it, wary, and he grinned and took one small step toward her, the food held out like an offering of peace. "Go on. It's not poisoned. I just bought it from the store not twenty minutes ago."

"What is it?"

His grin widened. "An apple."

Apple. She knew the word, one of the hundreds she'd read in her father's books but never really understood because such things didn't exist in the permanent snow and ice of Dusk.

She took the apple from his offering hand and twisted it around between her own, examining it from every angle. "How do you…?"

"Bite it."

Ember obeyed, taking a small chunk out of the side of the apple. The skin snapped between her teeth, barely a barrier at all, and a sweet, sharp flavor, unlike anything she was familiar with, bloomed inside her mouth.

She took another, larger bite. The apple had a delightful soft crunch.

When she finished chewing and swallowing a couple of bites, she turned her attention back to Felix, who was grinning at her, obviously amused. "Good?" he asked.

"Very. Where do you get such things?"

"They grow in the fields east of town."

He said it so casually as if *growing things* was just the normal course of life, and she felt kind of foolish for being so amazed by it.

She'd expected Frost to be different than Dusk. It was a city that maybe didn't even exist, full of people who maybe were just the souls of the dead — of course, it would be different. But at every turn so far, the realization of *how* different things in this city actually were kept slamming her in the face.

People who weren't trying to rob or kill her would come up behind her in the street to say hello. Buildings were made of wood and glass. There was warmth and light. Food *grew* here.

It was staggering and, frankly, a bit upsetting. Ember and Eli and everyone either of them had ever known —

they all had next to nothing. Dwindling rations of food and light, all of it carefully controlled by the elders, and none of it enough to do more than barely scrape by. And here was Frost, with its conspicuous abundance — so much that a boy Ember had only just met offered her food without a hint of worry about where his own next meal might come from.

"Is there someone showing you around?" Felix asked after a moment, interrupting her thoughts.

"No."

"Oh." His expression brightened subtly again. "Do you want there to be? I'm not as good a guide as my father would be — he could take you all around the palace — but … I can show you around a little. If you want," he added, probably in response to the frown spreading across Ember's face. "Only if you want."

Did she want a guide? She wasn't entirely sure. He could probably show her things she wouldn't think to look for and answer some of her questions, but could she trust him to not lead her into a trap?

She looked him over for what was probably the dozenth time. There was no guile in his eyes, only a spark of hope, a warm and friendly smile, and it occurred to her that he might be as interested in showing her around as she was in looking around.

Ember pulled in a breath, weighing her desire against her suspicion. Perhaps, in this case, Eli was right, and the people of Frost didn't need to live in fear of others. Felix certainly didn't seem afraid of her, even though she'd been one stupid oversight away from sticking a knife in his belly.

She wasn't ready to head back to the apartment. She still wanted to look around and maybe even find out something about the city they'd stumbled into. And she was fairly confident that she could hold her own in a fight if Felix tried something.

She let out her breath. "Alright," she said, more as a sigh than a word. "Yes. Show me around."

She smiled, and Felix's face lit up like the sun emerging from behind a cloud.

Chapter Eight

EMBER MUNCHED on her apple as she followed Felix around the square.

"This is the town's main square. You can get to the palace by going two blocks that way." He waved in the direction she'd come from.

A crunch on her apple. She'd gotten down to a thin strip in the middle that was studded with seeds.

They passed the Atalanta statue again; without pausing in his steps, Felix leaned to one side and brushed his finger-tips across the smooth place at the statue's feet where her name had been worn almost entirely away by thousands of similar gestures. He barely seemed to notice himself doing it, like the way Eli's mother Asha rubbed at her prayer bead with Atalanta's name on it, an unconscious sort of fidget.

Ember glanced toward the statue's face again. Light sparkled against the glass of the other buildings and the Atalanta statue, and her breath caught at the sight of it.

Felix looked at her, grinning again. His eyes flickered

up toward the sky. "Just wait. The moon will be up soon. You've never seen anything like Atalanta in moonlight."

"I've never seen anything like anything here."

He reached into his bag and offered her another apple. "You didn't tell me where you're from."

"North," she said, hoping that was vague enough.

"Well, of course north."

Ember book a bite of her fresh apple. Something about the way he said those words raised her suspicions again. "Why 'of course north'?"

Felix gave her a look. In the low light, she couldn't decide what that look was supposed to mean. "There's no other direction you could've come from. Our outer wall runs the entire way east to west."

"What about south?"

The smile slipped from his face, leaving his expression oddly blank. "There is no south."

Ember made a confused noise that never quite formed into a word. She'd never seen anyone's face change like that so fast.

But Felix only repeated the words like saying them would make them true. "There is no south of Frost."

She looked away, uncomfortable under the sudden blankness in his stare. "Dusk," she said at last.

And, just as fast as it had come, the blankness was gone, replaced by his smile. "Dusk," he repeated, saying the word with the tenderness of a lover speaking the name of his beloved. "What's it like?"

Ember snorted. Imagine a Frost boy wanting to know about Dusk! But when she looked back at him, the curiosity in his eyes hadn't dimmed.

This was perhaps the strangest thing of all the strange things about this place. She'd expected suspicion and wariness from everyone inside the walls. Hostility. Perhaps even interrogation and imprisonment. Those things made sense to her. But interest? Curiosity? Maybe eventually, after she'd found her way inside the city, but certainly not as she was first setting foot on the street from the random boy she'd met in the crowd.

"I don't know," Ember said at last when Felix remained quiet and eager. "Dusk is … cold. Dark. Dying. No one wants to admit it, but everyone knows our rations are running out. We've been living on a decreasing supply of food and warmth and light since … well, since Before."

"Before?"

"You know. *Before*."

His eyebrows pulled together, making visible creases in his forehead and a single deep line between his brows, just over the bridge of his nose.

"Before the death of the Engine. Before all of this." She waved her hand up at the sky, the cold, the snow and ice that pressed up against the outside of Frost's walls. She'd never met anyone who didn't understand "Before" — it was such a universal concept in her world.

But the frown on Felix's face didn't change.

She wasn't sure what to make of this. He himself was too young to have been alive Before, so of course, he wouldn't remember it, but surely there were people in the city — his parents, perhaps, or certainly his grandparents — who remembered, who told stories of Steppe when it was green and flourishing.

People who actually remembered such things were few and far between, and increasingly so as the years passed, but in a city this big, surely there were dozens, maybe hundreds, of people old enough to remember. Did they not talk about it? Were there no books that described it?

How could Felix have no concept of Before?

But she sensed that to press this issue would be rude, so she filed that question away to ask later.

They left the square behind and merged in with the crowd at a different spot than where Ember had come from. There was direction to Felix's steps, and he moved with the speed and decisiveness of purpose, eating up the ground with a stride that had Ember nearly jogging to keep up with.

The streets were lit now with small glass bulbs set at regular intervals at the tops of metal poles. As Ember passed beneath one, she could hear a faint but distinctive hum coming from the bulb. She stopped, distracted from the effort of keeping up with her local guide. Her bare fingers touched the pole with the gentle reverence of Atalanta worshipers brushing fingers across her name.

Felix noticed that she had paused and looped back to her. She smiled at him. "Electric?"

He smiled back, amused. "Of course."

Questions bubbled in her mind. How did Frost distribute electricity? Where was it produced? She didn't know much about electricity — Dusk never had it — but that only made her want to understand. The machines needed to make usable electricity were supposed to be large and complicated. Surely they couldn't be hidden, even in a city this size. Were they something Felix would be able to show her?

She settled with, "Do you know about electricity?"

No point in getting her hopes up if Felix wasn't someone to ask about it.

He squinted up at the bulb. "Not really. These lights are triggered by the dark, same as in the palace, I think."

"What about the machines that make it? Where are those?"

"Machines?" he repeated, with the same confused frown he'd worn for the mention of Before.

"There must be machines. Probably great big ones. Do you know where they are?"

He shook his head slowly, not understanding. "It's not machines that make all this. It's the queen."

This pulled her attention down to him. "The queen?"

"Yeah, her magic. It's why we have everything we have. Everything inside the walls is thanks to her. The warmth and light, the food. Even the electricity."

Ember frowned. "How's that possible?"

He shrugged as though the answer to that question was the least interesting thing in the world. "It's magic. C'mon." His tone flipped back to enthusiastic, and his smile returned as though it had never left. "I wanna show you the old city. It's my favorite place."

She followed, but her thoughts were trapped back at the first electric bulb. Her father used to say that magic was just science that wasn't understood, but clearly, someone somewhere in the city understood electricity. Someone had to have built and maintained the machine that created and distributed the electricity.

But Felix didn't seem to even understand what she meant when she asked about them. He didn't even seem curious, even though he'd been just about bursting when he asked about Dusk. The difference was so complete and obvious. It was like someone had toggled a switch inside him.

Here are the things you can be curious about; here are the things you can't be.

But, again, Ember sensed that to press would be rude, and Felix's friendly, talkative switch had flipped back on anyway. "The old city is on the south side of town, but I think there's a trolley stop at the next corner."

He frowned at the intersection ahead, his eyes focusing on a small pattern of little glittering circles arranged into a small triangle, and his expression brightened again. "Yes, the Queen's Line. That'll take us to the cathedral." He smiled at her. "You thought the square was impressive? Just wait until you see the cathedral."

They paused at the next intersection, moving a little ways toward the nearest building, where a handful of other people stood in a loose clump facing south down the north-south road. One or two of them glanced their way as they joined the group. They caught Ember's eye, smiled wide, bobbed their heads, then turned away again with their smiles still firmly in place.

Ember turned her attention to Felix. "What's a cathedral?"

"It's a building."

"Like these?"

He nodded. "Only bigger — and much older. It's got this domed roof that ..." His words faded, and he held out his arm, covered now in the tiny bumps that people in Dusk called gooseflesh, which Ember had intuited was some kind of comment on the way a bird looked when plucked. Not that she knew what a bird looked like, plucked or otherwise. "It gives me the shivers just thinking about it."

"You like buildings?"

"Architecture, yeah. There's something about the way we used to build buildings that's been lost since we started using glass instead of wood or brick. Mind you, I'm not saying it wasn't the right thing to do," he added with a furtive glance toward the other people nearby, a glance that Ember suspected she wasn't supposed to see. "Obviously, Frost would've never become what it is if we hadn't made the change. But I still like the old city."

One of the people in the crowd shifted. It was a man pushing up against the others, jostling them enough to tug at the crowd's attention. Ember glanced at him — he was one of the smiling people. He met her eyes and beamed, pushed again to take a few extra steps toward her.

Ember shifted away, fresh suspicion washing through her. She didn't like the look of the man's smile — it was too big, like so many of the Frost people's smiles, but there was something else behind it, a strange, almost unhinged expression buried beneath the stretched-tight lips and gleaming white teeth.

The man didn't seem to notice her pulling away, but Felix did. He caught the man's eyes and frowned a little. "Something wrong?" he asked, his voice newly flat.

The man didn't take his eyes or smile from Ember. He leaned forward and whispered to her under his breath. "The wall is cracking."

Ember took another step back, letting Felix come between her and the smiling man. Her fingers ached for the heft and safety of her knife but closed around empty air instead.

"Step back," she hissed.

The man froze, but his eyes and smile didn't waver, didn't stray from the place on her face they'd latched themselves onto. When she took another step away from him, though, he remained where he was — not stepping away, but not pursuing her, either.

A rumble of wheels echoed down the street, and by the time Ember had turned her head in the direction of the sound, a squarish open-sided vehicle had pulled to a stop at the intersection. The driver at the front yanked back on a lever that must've been some kind of brake and nodded to the loose clump of people at the intersection. One by one, they stepped onto the doorless step into the vehicle, dropped a coin into the small glass box sitting at the driver's right hand, and took a seat among the dozen or so empty ones inside the vehicle.

Felix touched Ember's elbow, encouraging her to follow him into the vehicle. He dropped two coins into the driver's machine. They clunked as they fell through the slit in the top and again, softer as they hit the small pile of coins at the bottom of the box, and Ember was suddenly very aware of how little she understood of the workings of the city.

"You don't have to pay for me," she whispered as she followed Felix toward the back of the trolley.

But he only shook his head and sat. "It's my pleasure. Do you want another apple? Or..." He glanced down at the bag. "I've got apricots and plums, too."

Ember sat beside him. "That's okay. But thank you."

"Anytime."

The trolley pulled away from the intersection. Unable to help herself, Ember glanced back toward where they'd left the strange man at the intersection. Three men in pressed white suits and gleaming black shoes surrounded him, their hands tight around his arms. He yelled something, but the words were lost to the rumble of the trolley.

Ember turned away and tried to dismiss the strangeness of the encounter.

The air spun around inside of the trolley, rippling hems and hair; Ember had to keep shoving her own wayward black strands out of her eyes. Glass buildings and electric lights blurred together as they passed street after street, sometimes stopping to exchange passengers.

Felix would occasionally point to one building or another. "That's the main office of Envoys. My father's head of the doll division and he mostly works at the palace, but sometimes, if they've got a new doll ..." He squinted at one of the spots along the glass exterior for a moment as the final passenger paid and sat down, then he leaned back and shrugged. "Well, he's not there now. But that's where his desk is."

Or: "That's the theater. You've probably never seen a moving picture?"

Ember shook her head.

Felix smiled. "It's closed now, but you'll have to go some time. They'll make you laugh, or cry, or scream, or whatever it is you want to feel at the moment."

This was interesting enough that Ember didn't want to let it go as the trolley zipped by the building. "How does it do that?"

"Oh, it's more of the queen's magic. Like the electricity, you know?"

She didn't, but the reference to the queen's magic shut down any further questions about moving pictures.

As the trolley continued through the Frost streets, the number of people getting off increased, and the number getting on dropped, and by the time Felix mentioned the next stop would be theirs, they were the only ones besides the driver left on it.

"The route loops around the old city before going back downtown," he said. "We should be able to catch it on its way back. That'll give us about twenty minutes — which I know isn't long, but I don't want you to think I'm trying to kidnap you."

Ember grinned. That worry had left her head by the time they'd gotten on the trolley. She wasn't sure why — it was still entirely possible that Felix was just hoping to lure her away from the crowds. But she realized that she trusted him. Perhaps that should worry her — he was still a stranger, a Frost boy taking her around a strange city — but it didn't. "Just go ahead and try," she said, her voice teasing. "I'd knock you flat and be back in my bed before you even came to."

"I believe you," he answered a hint of laughter in his voice.

The trolley slowed. They'd left the busyness of the palace square well behind, and the electric lights appeared much dimmer as the amount of glass around them lessened from full buildings to just windows and doors. At the intersection where the trolley was preparing to stop, a few people waited, and a few more people sat at a smattering of small round tables and sipped steaming beverages out of white porcelain teacups.

Felix stood. "Here we are."

Ember followed him off the trolley and then down a road that was much narrower than the streets around the palace and not quite as well-lit. The air was noticeably colder here, too, as though the force field was weaker this far away from the palace. The buildings were wood and just a bit fallen down. Not quite decrepit, but without the shining newness of the other buildings she'd seen in the city.

Weathered, Ember decided. The wooden buildings around here had stood for a long time, and they were showing their age.

And then, much like it had in front of the palace, the street spit them out into an open space lit silver with moonlight.

Ember sucked in a breath. The square had certainly been a sight, and she couldn't imagine how glorious it might be to see now, but this ... this was something else entirely.

It was the cathedral. She didn't need Felix to tell her that, though he did whisper it with reverence. Ember didn't know what cathedrals were supposed to be like, but this was certainly it.

It was massive, not as tall as the tallest spires of the palace, but much wider, and made of material she didn't recognize. It gleamed like fresh snow and was capped by a dome in great stripes of color that wound in an increasingly tight spiral as they twisted from the building to the peak in its center.

"It used to be the altar to Mother Atalanta," Felix said. His voice was still barely louder than a breath, and when she looked over at him, she saw that his arms were once again speckled with gooseflesh. "People would come from every part of the city to worship and pray. The priestesses lived in the dome."

"Used to?" Ember whispered back.

He smiled sadly. "The altar moved to the palace after it was built, and the priestesses live in an apartment in the square now."

"Why?"

He looked down at her like she was asking a stupid question again. "To be closer to Our Mother."

Ember felt something snap into place, an understanding forming out of the messy confusion in her thoughts.

The queen, whoever she really was, whatever she could really do, had the people in Frost believing that she was Atalanta.

Ember had never been particularly religious — her father had taught her to be skeptical, and to him, that extended to being skeptical of religious claims as well. But Dusk was overall pretty religious, and Ember could see what the queen must've wanted to do by claiming that she was Atalanta, moving the altar and priestesses, putting a statue in her square.

She was trying to tell the people of Frost that she was their goddess.

Ember shook off the thought. She didn't have anything else to do with it, and there was something much more interesting facing her right now to think about. She took a step toward the cathedral. "So what's in it now?"

Chapter Nine

"I DON'T THINK we're supposed to go in there."

Ember agreed. It wasn't the sort of place that looked especially inviting or like it would be okay to step inside and have a look around, but she couldn't help wanting a closer look. The cathedral was magnificent from the outside, perhaps the most magnificent thing she'd ever seen, and she couldn't understand why getting a little closer to it would be a bad thing.

"You've never gone in?" she asked conversationally, as she stepped toward the cathedral.

Felix followed behind her, the reverence in his voice shifting into nervousness. "I ... no. Of course not."

She glanced over at him, one eyebrow raised at the obvious lie in his voice.

He grimaced, caught. His eyes swept the area around him as if confirming that they were alone, then smiled just a little, with just the corners of his lips. "Well, just the once. When I was little. I only peeked through the window. There wasn't anything there but a big empty room. Couldn't even see the dome from there."

Ember was close enough to the building now to search for a window. There were several low enough to see through, and in the moonlight, they looked like mosaics of glass colors. She ran one finger across the bottom of the nearest, liking the cool, smooth touch of glass against her fingertips, the little bumps where one colored piece was joined up with another and melted smooth.

"We don't have glass in Dusk, except for the trinkets that have survived from Before," she murmured, almost to herself. Then, recalling that Felix somehow didn't have a concept of "Before," she added, "They're really old. From our grandmother's grandmother's generation at least."

"What do you put in your windows?"

She laughed. "What windows?"

"You don't have windows?"

"A window is just a fancy word for a hole in your house where all the heat can escape."

"Huh." Felix glanced at the window they were in front of now, another of the multi-colored mosaic ones. "No windows. No wonder you all go mad."

"Mad?" Ember repeated.

"Not you, I mean," Felix added, his face growing flushing. "Just … you know. Outlanders in general. Before they become dragons, they go mad?"

His last word tilted up until it became unmistakably a question. But it wasn't the mad part that was confusing — it was that strange word he used, "dragon."

It sounded almost familiar, tugging at Ember's attention like a forgotten dream, like a word she used to know but could no longer remember where she'd seen it or what it meant.

She turned toward the window again, knocking the itchy sense of missing something away. Dragons could wait; the cathedral couldn't.

The coloring of the glass, the mosaic construction, plus the dim silvery moonlight, made it hard to see clearly through, but Ember squinted, determined to see past the colors and her own reflection into the building itself.

She wasn't sure what she expected to see — probably just a large empty room like Felix said, or maybe the inevitable dingy chairs and cold, ashy fireplace of a long-abandoned space.

What she saw was neither of those things.

It was a large space, the walls stretching into darkness to both the right and forward — less to the left because she wasn't far from the front door, a massive, elaborately carved piece of wood worth attention in its own right. But it wasn't empty. It was full practically to bursting.

What it was full *of*, though, Ember couldn't tell.

They were clearly machines of some sort, with rounded metal fronts and protruding tails on the back. At the very top of the rounded area were jumbles of gears and belts clearly meant to serve some kind of purpose, but the room was too dark, and she was too far away to even hazard a guess at what the machines did.

Felix leaned in to look, too, apparently over the uncertainty of whether they should be here, at least enough to once again take a look inside. "Are those ... copters?"

Ember wanted to take a closer look. There were a dozen of them or more, all lined up neatly in the room but smashed so close together that some of their gears touched their neighbor's. She traced what she could see of the nearest one's gears, trying to figure out what they were for. "What are copters?"

"They're broken," Felix said like it was an answer. "But ... why?"

He backed away then, and when Ember didn't follow

him, he reached for her sleeve and tugged. "We really shouldn't be here."

Ember frowned. He'd been the one to bring her out here, and now he wanted to go back, just like that? Because the cathedral was full of broken copters?

He readjusted his grip so now he had her elbow, too, not hard, but with a firmness that was impossible to ignore.

Fear shot like ice through Ember's veins. Had she been wrong to trust him? Was he going to harm her now?

Fist to the nose, elbow to the belly, knee to the groin. She tried to calculate the distance between them and the nearest lit intersection a quick sprint away.

But when she jerked her arm free, he let it go without a fight. "C'mon. The trolley will be back around in a few minutes."

He stepped back toward the street, away from the cathedral and the broken copters inside it.

"WHO WOULD STUFF a room full of broken machines?"

The trolley had indeed come back around a few minutes after they returned to the corner. Felix had paid the driver again, even though it was the same driver they'd seen just a few minutes before, and there was no way he didn't recognize the fire-haired boy and the strangely dressed girl that got aboard.

But the driver's eyes were vacant, the only spark in them coming from the too-big smile he gave them as the coins dropped into his collection box.

They'd taken the same seat they'd had on the way up here, and after a couple of trolley stops and a few more passengers, the stiffness in Felix's shoulders began to relax. Now, almost back to the stop where they'd first gotten on, Ember asked the question.

"I don't know what you're talking about," Felix answered.

"The copters. They were broken, but why?"

"They…" He hesitated and shot a glance around the trolley. Most of the other passengers were engaged in their own low-voiced conversations — only one, a woman, met Felix's eyes and smiled.

He faced the front of the trolley. His fingers tightened subtly into each other on his lap. "I don't know what you're asking."

"You do so. You asked the same thing, about why—"

"No." He spun halfway around toward her and fixed her with a look that seemed to carry a significance she didn't understand. "I didn't see anything, and neither did you."

"But—"

"Ember," he interrupted with absolute seriousness, his voice falling to a whisper, "you didn't see anything inside the cathedral. Just a big empty room." His eyes flashed once more toward the smiling woman, who only smiled wider, showing teeth. "Right?"

"Oh. Right," she agreed slowly. Maybe it was just the intensity of his own stare that made her feel like she was being watched.

She glanced at the smiling woman, too, and suddenly wondered if letting it go was quite enough. "Sorry. Sometimes I … make things up. Outworlder, you know."

Felix nodded once, a short, almost invisible nod, then smiled wide and deliberate, and his voice went almost a little too loud, as though he wanted to be heard clearly over the rumble of the trolley's wheels. "The old city's not entirely abandoned, obviously, but when the queen moved the altar to the palace, it fell out of favor with the businesses that were supported by worshipers. It can be annoying to take a trolley all the way out there to buy food."

There was a new tone in his voice now, an overly pedantic one that had her thinking his words were more for the trolley passengers than they were for her.

Ember tried to school her expression into polite, but not excessive, curiosity and reached for something that might be safer than whatever was spooking him about the copters in the cathedral. "So the food moved toward the palace?"

"Right."

The trolley pulled up to the intersection where they'd first gotten on. Felix stood and led Ember back onto the street. The strange formal tone melted back into what she was starting to think was his normal warm, interested voice. "Do you need me to show you back?"

She shook her head. "That's not necessary. I can find it."

His grin slipped a little. She could see him struggle to catch it before it vanished entirely, and when he did, it was much smaller and more forced than before. "Are you sure? I wouldn't want you to get lost."

"I won't. I'm good at finding my way around."

"Okay." Another slip of his grin, another catch before it disappeared entirely. "It's been fun."

"It has," Ember agreed, meaning it. "Thank you."

He dropped his hand and looked down at his feet. One boot scuffed at the street beneath it, and his pale cheeks flushed to almost the same color as his hair. "Can I see you again?" he asked without looking up.

Ember smiled, hopefully hiding the way her own face began to feel unusually warm at the question. "I'd like that."

Felix glanced up at her without lifting his head. A

twitch at one corner of his mouth made it clear he was trying to still a grin. "Really?"

She nodded. "Really."

The momentarily stilled grin broke through his hold on it, and he beamed at her, the smile as bright as the electric lights casting a halo of red around his face. "Okay. I'll see you around, then?"

"Yeah."

She hurried away before she could say anything more but glanced back once before turning down the next street. Felix was watching her, still beaming. He lifted one hand in a silent wave as she went around the corner.

IT WAS no trouble to find the Queen's Cross Cafe, and from there the building with the matte-black metal staircase and the hallway lined with doors. She slid into the room and closed the door softly behind her, not wanting to wake Eli, who she figured was still asleep in the next room.

"Where have you been?"

She jumped and spun around, though the moment she did, she realized it wasn't necessary. The voice was Eli's, and it was only because she hadn't expected to find him behind her that he'd startled her.

He was sitting on the couch, but he stood, his arms crossed, when she turned to face him. His expression was accusatory, almost angry.

Ember lifted her chin. "I told you. I was going for a walk."

"A walk? Ember, you've been gone for hours!"

"You could've come with me."

Eli let out a breath and unfolded his arms. "I was worried."

"Why? You're the one who's been trying to convince me that there's nothing to be worried about."

She started to move past him, aiming for the door that lead into the bedroom, but he came after her, grabbing her arm when she didn't stop to look at him. "Where've you been?" he asked again, gentler this time.

"Out. Seeing the city. That thing I would've thought was your interest."

He didn't rise to the bait, instead asking evenly, "What did you see?"

"Lots of things. People, buildings. The palace. They have electricity here." She glanced out the glass wall to her left, and yes, she could see the nearest light pole, shining a steady bluish light onto the cobbles and glass around it. "Did you see those bulbs? They're *electric*!"

He was quiet for a moment, looking at her through slightly narrowed eyes. "Anything else?"

She reflected his expression back to him. "Are you being suspicious of me?" She wasn't sure why she didn't want to tell him about Felix or the old city. There was nothing to tell him about the cathedral or the things inside it.

But Felix felt like her own thing, and not even the least bit of Eli's business.

His face cleared. "Of course not."

"Good." She smiled and pulled her arm away from his hand, but then tried to disguise the motion by reaching up and patting his cheek in the way that annoyed him the most. "Otherwise, I would have to kick your ass."

He moved away from her hand, but he was grinning now, too. "You think you could take me?"

"I know I could."

Mischief glinted in his eyes.

Ember took a step back. "Don't."

He lowered his head and closed the two steps of distance between them at an awkward not-quite-run. His arms went around her in a playful facsimile of an attack, and his momentum sent them both stumbling into the side wall of the room.

"You're such a little boy," Ember said, but she was laughing, and that softened the scolding edge of her words.

"Someone has to keep you from becoming a mean old woman before your time," Eli said. His voice cracked over his own laughter.

She slapped his shoulder. "Get off me."

He laughed again but let her go.

"Do you feel better now?"

"Yes."

"Am I allowed to go to bed? I'd like to look my best while paying tribute to the queen." Those last words came out of her with a faint but hopefully detectable bite of sarcasm.

Felix had told her to think of it as saying hello to her host, but there was something about the phrase of "paying tribute" that made her uneasy.

Eli waved a hand toward the bedroom as if to say she could do whatever she wanted.

Ember pulled off her sweater and kicked off her boots, then lay down in the bed farthest from the glass wall. A few minutes later, she heard Eli crawl into the one at the center of the room, and a few minutes after that, the deep, steady breaths that meant he was asleep. He'd always been the sort of person who could just go straight to sleep pretty much the moment he lay down, as though he never had anything on his mind.

But Ember couldn't fall asleep. The bed was delightful: as soft as a cloud, with a thick and equally soft blanket and *two* pillows so fluffy she doubted anyone had ever put their head on them. None of it was thermal, but maybe that shouldn't have surprised her — she hadn't seen a speck of thermal anywhere in Frost, which might actually be all right since they had a force field over the city and plenty of heat indoors to keep them all from freezing to death without it.

Still, despite the comfort of the bed and the drowsy noises of Eli just a few steps away, she couldn't relax enough to sleep. Her thoughts ran over all the things she'd seen and heard during the day, and they kept getting snarled on the strange way Felix's eager curiosity kept changing to indifference or denial over questions that seemed completely innocent and reasonable to her. Where did Frost keep the machines that made the electricity that lit its streets? Why did the queen move Atalanta's altar out of the old city? How was there someone who didn't understand what she meant when she mentioned Before?

What were copters, and why did they spook Felix?

It was that last question that kept circling back to her, even as she was able to dismiss the rest with the idea that maybe Felix just wasn't interested in machines. Which wasn't at all unreasonable — there were things she didn't care about, and if someone were to ask her a question about those things, she wouldn't know or feel inclined to answer. But Felix had called the old city his favorite place, and even the thought of the cathedral gave him shivers. He hadn't been afraid when he'd taken her into the trolley or down the street to point out the building. He'd only started to get nervous when he saw the copters.

He didn't want anyone in the trolley knowing that either of them had seen anything, but he also didn't tell her what she had seen.

It was all just a little too suspicious for Ember to dismiss.

Chapter Ten

EMBER DREAMED of the end of the world.

She knew she was dreaming from the moment she opened her dream-self eyes and looked around her to see nothing but white in every direction. It wasn't like the whiteout that had preceded their discovering that they'd made it to Frost — it wasn't a whiteness made by snow and wind. It was the whiteness of nothing.

This was surprising. She'd always thought of nothing as being dark. Black. An absence of light like the space between the stars.

But this was something else. It wasn't light — at least, she didn't feel compelled to squint against the glare — but it wasn't dark, either. It was just … nothing.

There was someone beside her. She turned, expecting to find Eli, and was surprised by the shock of fiery orange that cut through the absolute whiteness around her.

"Felix," she said, her dream-voice echoing strangely in the void.

He didn't turn. His eyes were fixed on something straight ahead, over her shoulder and to the right, but when Ember tried to see what he was looking at, there was nothing there.

Nothing but nothing.

Here there be dragons.

She knew that phrase. But she couldn't figure out where she knew it from, or why it kept banging around inside her skull like something she was supposed to know and didn't. It just sat there, humming beneath her consciousness, drawn up in her dreams, impossible to understand or place.

Felix had made a reference to dragons outside of Frost's walls. She didn't really know the word dragon, didn't really have any concept of what he meant — something about monsters, she thought, monsters who had been driven snow-blind and insane from being out in the unprotected tundra. But still the words echoed, meaningful but unable to be grasped. Half-remembered like the sensation of a dream fading out of consciousness.

Ember woke with a start. For a moment, she wasn't sure where she was; all she could see was white, as though she were still trapped inside the void of her dream. There was something wrapped around her body, pinning her arms to her sides. She yelped and kicked out, but the thing only tightened.

"Ember? It's okay, it's me."

Eli pierced the whiteness in front of her eyes, and it all came rushing back to her. The trek across the tundra, Frost, the too-soft bed and too-white blanket. She dropped her head back against the thick pillow with a sigh.

"Bad dream?"

She tried to laugh in an effort to dislodge the panic still caught in a fist-sized lump in her throat. "You'd think I'd be used to them by now."

He rubbed her shoulder where his hand was already

resting, and she realized that he must've been shaking her awake. "Get up," he said, straightening. "Maudie's here."

"Ugh. Why?"

"To take you to the queen," said Maudie's too-cheerful voice through her too-big smile. "You have an appointment at sunrise."

Ember didn't groan, though the urge to was strong. Instead, she rolled out of bed and landed barefoot on the floor.

Eli stepped away from the edge of her bed. He'd changed at some point since they'd gone to bed, and now he was in the light pants and sleeveless top of a Frost man, the hat held in one hand.

Ember scoffed. "You look ridiculous."

"Maybe. But it's very comfortable." He gave a little shimmy of his hips. The motion swirled the loose hems of his shirt and pants. "Don't look so horrified until you see what Maudie brought for you."

Maudie, who'd been standing at the doorway to the bedroom and smiling brightly at nothing, stepped forward at the sound of her name. Folded up in her outstretched arms was a piece of white cloth and a wide-brimmed hat perched on top.

Ember stepped away from the offering as though it were poisoned. "I'm not wearing that."

"The queen requested that you be decent when you arrive."

Ember looked down at the thick knitted sweater and pants that she hadn't bothered to take off when she went to bed last night. She couldn't have possibly been more decent, especially compared to Maudie's exposed ankles and bare shoulders.

Eli took the bundle from Maudie's arms. "I'll take care of it," he said like a dismissal.

Maudie's smile seemed to thin, like it was a moment away from breaking. Ember was tempted to push it, to find out what the other woman looked like when she finally got angry enough to stop smiling. But then Maudie turned away from the door her foot had been propping open, and it snapped quietly closed between them.

Ember turned to Eli. "I'm not wearing that."

Eli sighed. "Don't argue. You'll just get yourself in trouble."

"I thought they didn't care what I did."

He still wouldn't take her bait. Instead, he dumped the cloth and wide-brimmed hat into her arms and said evenly, "Come out when you've changed."

Then he followed Maudie out of the room and shut the door behind him. She could hear him talking on the other side of the door, his voice too low for her to make out any specific words.

Ember scowled down at the clothes. She didn't want to wear them, but she didn't really want to argue with Eli, either. The last few weeks, it felt like pretty much all they'd done was argue. Over whether or not she'd leave with him. Over supplies to take. Over if his quest to find this maybe-mythical city was a stupid suicide mission. Over how long each day they could walk. Over the strangeness she'd seen from the people in Frost. Over how long she'd been away yesterday. It was exhausting, and she didn't want to do it anymore, especially over something as trivial as clothing.

She let out a breath, long and careful, emptying her lungs as completely as she could before filling them all the way back up again. It wasn't like they were taking her own clothes away. She could put on Frost garments for a little while to get through this one errand, and then change back into her own clothes afterward. So she changed, folding her sweater and pants and laying them neatly on the end of her bed — they weren't manufactured thermals that needed special care, but they were wool, knitted by her father's mother, the grandmother from Before that she'd never met, from her own small flock of sheep, because apparently, even before, it would get cold enough in the winter to want a warm sweater. Even the great Engine couldn't keep everywhere free of dark and snow.

The Frost clothes were surprisingly comfortable; the linen of the dress was light and soft, and though she felt exposed and naked with her extremities out in the air, it wasn't entirely unpleasant. She liked the way the knee-length skirt moved when she did, and she liked how her dark arms and calves stood out against the white fabric.

She felt ... pretty. Exposed, embarrassed, worried about the skin that only rarely and briefly had direct contact with air, but also pretty.

It was a strange feeling, and one that she tried to fight down before she opened the door and went out to meet Eli and Maudie.

Both of them looked at her with smiles when she came out of the bedroom. Maudie's was bright and plastered on as usual, but Eli's was almost appreciative. "Frost suits you, Ember," he muttered.

"Don't get used to it," she muttered back.

Maudie opened the door into the hallway and waved them out after her. "Come. We mustn't be late for the queen."

Ember and Eli followed her without a word; from the corner of her eye, Ember could see Eli still shimmying around inside the new clothes, taking too-large steps or holding out his arms as if testing the limits of the cloth. Ember kept her arms firmly down at her sides, hoping that keeping them in toward her body would keep the exposed skin warm and the skirt from shifting around too much and showing off parts it was supposed to be covering.

The air outside the building was biting, far too cold for the thin linen and amount of skin it failed to cover. Maudie's steps quickened, and Ember was plenty eager now to keep up. There were a dozen intersections between here and the palace square — the faster they could cover them, the sooner they'd be back inside.

But Maudie turned away from the street Ember had taken yesterday into the square, led them up the street past the Queen's Cross Cafe, then paused at the next corner near a small collection of others, all loosely gathered and looking in the same direction like a group waiting for the next trolley.

And indeed, just a few minutes later, a trolley came rumbling up the street. Beside her, Ember heard Eli pull in a breath, and she remembered that it was Felix, not Eli, who'd taken her on the trolley last night.

She smiled. "Just wait until you see how fast it goes."

He looked at her, eyebrows raised. "You've been on one?"

"You should've come with me yesterday. I did all sorts of things you wish you'd had a chance to do."

The trolley stopped at the corner, several people hopping off and the small crowd waiting for it replacing them. Maudie dropped three coins into the driver's little metal box and then led them to two open seats in the middle. "Take those," she said, pointing. "I'll fetch you when we get to our stop."

Ember sat and tugged Eli down beside her. The driver disengaged the brake lever, and the trolley rolled forward to its next stop.

Eli stared out the open side of the vehicle, his jaw

slightly loose with awe as the buildings whipped by at a speed at least twice as fast as a dead run. Ember fought back an urge to giggle. She probably hadn't looked much more dignified on last night's trolley ride, and Felix hadn't laughed at her. It seemed only right that she extend Eli the same courtesy.

Still, she couldn't help but smile. "You going to catch a fly in that trap?" she whispered, teasing. It was a saying in Dusk, one of those that sounded like they meant something until you stopped to think about it and realized that it meant nothing at all.

The man sitting in the seat in front of them turned halfway around at her words. His smile was wide, but not overly so — more friendly than unnatural. "Where are you folks headed?" he asked.

Eli was able to pull his eyes off the passing buildings long enough to answer him. "The palace."

"Oh?" The man lifted his eyebrows. His expression went from politely idle to genuinely curious. "Got business there?"

"An appointment with the queen," Ember cut in.

The man's smile never faltered. He made a small noise somewhere in his throat and immediately turned around to face the front of the trolley again.

The trip wasn't long — they weren't going far. Ember had strolled the distance between the apartment and the palace in less than an hour, and though they stopped frequently and were taking a route that was much more winding than the one she'd done yesterday, the trolley was more than a mite faster than her strolling. Between the buildings and down the open stretches of street, Ember could begin to see the vast mountain that sat behind the palace, and then, after a few more stops and one new turn, the bluish spires of the palace and open square in front of it.

The trolley pulled up to a corner immediately in front of the square, and Maudie started toward the front door of the vehicle, once again gesturing for Ember and Eli to follow her. They did, and a few moments later, they'd joined the mild throng of people spilling into the square.

The sky was brightening with the approach of sunrise, the clouds, and even the sky itself, turning an unreal shade of purple in the dawn. Ember found herself staring at those clouds. She'd never seen anything like that color for a sunrise, and her mind struggled with it for a moment until she realized that the clouds weren't actually purple: they were red, and the blue tint of the force field between the clouds made them appear unnaturally purple.

Eli paused at the Atalanta statue as they passed it. He pressed his fingers to his lips and then to the statue's feet, then spun back toward the palace and hurried to catch back up. "I haven't worshiped properly in a week," he muttered, though Ember wasn't sure if the words were for her or not.

"I'm sure she understands," Ember said back. After all, Atalanta was an explorer — there weren't many people quite as keen to follow her example as Eli.

"Still, as my mother used to say—"

"That's no excuse," she quoted with him.

"Exactly." He smiled like a grimace of guilt.

"We'll be back this way, I'm sure," Ember whispered. She didn't like that Eli felt guilty over having not paid tribute to the mythical person who may or may not have actually existed. "We'll make sure to stop once we're not on a schedule." She glanced meaningfully at Maudie's back; the other woman had nearly broken into a jog, and the gestures she'd made the last couple of minutes for her charges to follow had become increasingly hurried and desperate. "I think right now, we'd better keep up with our escort."

The front doors of the palace were separated from the square by a large chasm dug out of the ground and spanned by bridge made of the same kind of thick bluish glass of the wall on the east edge of the city. It was barely wide enough for two people to cross abreast. The number of people filing toward the palace now was significantly less than when she'd seen the place yesterday afternoon, but there were still enough people on the bridge that Ember wondered how it didn't crack and drop them into the crack in the ground. She glanced over the railing that ran the entire length of the bridge. The chasm they hurried over wasn't the biggest crack in the ground she'd ever seen — there was one not far from the walls of Dusk that ran from the top of its medium-sized glacier and fell for several hundred feet to the bottom. She'd once let Eli convince her to go there with him and even poked around the top of it, clinging to the sheer walls of ice around her with nothing but a pick and a short length of rope to keep her from falling in. This crack wasn't nearly as deep as that, nor as treacherous-looking on the sides; if she were to fall, she felt fairly certain that she'd be able to climb out with only the soft cloth boots that had come with her pile of Frost woman clothing.

Still, walking across such a place on a strip of glass felt like an unwise thing to risk. Even if she could climb out of the crack, the impact of the ground from the actual fall might very well kill her before she had a chance to test whether or not she could climb back out again.

Ember hurried across the bridge, grateful to see when she glanced over at Eli that he seemed to feel some of the same anxiety on the crossing.

Maudie had finally paused on the other side of the bridge. Her smile must've slipped some while she was walking because she had to readjust and smear it back on when Ember and Eli caught up to her. "All right?"

Ember nodded. Eli didn't answer; his attention seemed to have switched from the glass bridge to the palace and the huge sheer cliff of the mountain behind it.

"I'm so glad I don't have to cross that bridge often, thanks be to the queen," Maudie muttered conspiratorially. "Though if I worked at the palace, I would grow accustomed, of course."

"Of course," Ember echoed when Maudie paused for confirmation.

"Follow me, if you please. The sun will be up any minute." She turned toward the front door.

Two men dressed in white pants and white coats and each holding a long, thin spear flanked the large front doors of the palace. One gestured with his spear for Maudie to stop as they approached — not exactly pointing it at her, but moving it as though he was considering pointing it at her. "State your name and your business," he said. His voice was deep and gravelly; Ember wondered if he'd been chosen to guard the front doors for the intimidating sound of his voice alone, seeing as the rest of him was far less impressive. He was taller than she was, but that was hardly difficult   Eli could meet his eyes without having to look up — and weedier than most of the other Frost men she'd seen. He seemed to have trouble controlling the end of his spear.

Maudie straightened. "I'm Maudie, and I've brought our visitors to pay tribute to our queen."

The guards looked Ember, and then Eli, from the tops of their head to the bottoms of their feet, then the one who'd spoken nodded and pulled back his spear. "Proceed."

The quiet one pulled open the door for them, and Maudie stepped in and waved Ember and Eli after her. The door closed behind them with a dull, echoing thud.

Chapter Eleven

THEY WERE IN A LARGE HALLWAY, faintly blue like the force field and smooth as glass. The inside was colder than it had been outside, a chill that seemed to radiate from the walls and floors itself. Ember reached out and brushed the wall with her fingers; they came away cold and very slightly damp.

So there was something in this city that was built with ice — but it was ice without flaws or marks from where blocks had been stacked or tools had been used.

People moved through the hall, stepping carefully to keep from slipping in their insufficient cloth shoes whenever they weren't hurrying across the long white rug that covered the center of the hallway. They kept their voices low if they needed to speak, or just continued silently on when they didn't. None of them seemed particularly interested in their visitors.

Maudie gestured again for Ember and Eli to follow her, and the three of them hurried down the hall, keeping to the center rug for traction. At the end of the hall was a door, which Maudie knocked on. "Come," said a female voice from the other side of the door.

Ember suspected that this was the room where the queen was, and considering the way the queen made such an effort to intimidate anyone who came through her front doors, she was preparing to see something spectacular. She remembered the stories she'd been told when she was a child, old tales of queens and spirits and heroics. The queens of those tales — when there were queens in them — were grand and regal.

Ember didn't believe in magic, but from everything she'd seen, it was a disbelief that was becoming increasingly difficult to hold onto.

What she saw when Maudie opened the door was not what she expected.

It was a room. Not even a particularly large room — bigger than any room she'd seen in Dusk, but not much bigger than their apartment. The flawless blue ice of the hallway ended at the door; the room was made of white boards and large but worn-thin rugs. At the far side of the room was a wide wooden desk, and behind the desk was a woman.

The woman — Ember presumed this was the queen — was middle-aged, dark-haired, and dressed like any one of the hundreds of women outside of her front doors. Ember wondered if Frost women dressed like her to emulate her or if she dressed like them in order to seem more personable. Her skin was so pale Ember could see the network of faint blue veins running across her neck and jaw, and she emphasized that faint blue tinge with lips and eyes painted to match the color of the ice outside her door. She stood up from behind the desk as Maudie ushered the visitors into the room. "Ah, our young Dusk friends," she said, moving around the desk and approaching the center of the room, one hand outstretched as if to shake. "I'm sorry it's taken so long for this meeting." She hesitated a moment, then took Eli's hand in both of her own. "We don't get many visitors anymore."

She turned to Ember and took her hand in that same double-fisted grip. Her fingers were cold.

"Please, won't you come in. Maudie, fetch some seats for my visitors."

"Yes, my queen." Maudie bobbed her head, grinning wide enough to crack her lips again, and backed out of the room.

"Come in, my friends." The queen stepped back and gestured expansively toward her desk as though she wanted them to sit on the edge of it or something.

Ember glanced at Eli, not sure what to make of this greeting. Frost citizens had been unexpectedly friendly, if sometimes a bit off-putting, but this was something else entirely. Was this really the queen whose supposed magic made everything inside the city possible? Who powered the electricity and grew the food and maintained the force field that held in warmth enough to keep the streets clear of snow and ice? Was this the queen who made her visitors cross a slick glass bridge over a frightening chasm and whose guard demanded in a not-unintimidating voice to know their names and business before going into the palace? Who built a palace of ice butting up against sheer mountain cliffs as though she specifically meant to strike fear and awe into the hearts and minds of those who saw it? This woman, who was now smiling warmly and apologizing for making them wait two days before finally saying hello?

There had been plenty of strangeness in Frost, but this must be the strangest thing of all. The queen, who had done everything in her not-insubstantial power to make it clear she was to be feared and loved like Frost's own personal deity, who demanded that visitors come to her palace to pay her tribute, should not be such a seemingly polite, hospitable, *normal* woman.

But when Ember looked at Eli to see what he made of all this, she only saw her own confusion reflected back at her. Clearly, he was just as shaken by the unexpected reality before him as she was.

"You must forgive the mess," the queen said, turning to her desk and shuffling a couple of papers. Ember hadn't even noticed the desk or the papers on it — her whole attention was still too caught up on the queen to care about much else. "I think I've managed at last to find you both some useful employment." She glanced back. Her eyes were as dark as her hair, standing out almost disturbingly from her pale skin and blue-painted eyelids.

Maudie came back into the room, a small wooden chair tucked under each of her arms. She set them down just a step in front of the desk.

The queen smiled. "Thank you, Maudie. Please wait outside until you're summoned again."

Maudie's smile somehow, impossibly, widened. "Yes, my queen," she muttered and then backed out of the room again.

"Please sit," said the queen.

Eli obeyed, and, after a moment, Ember did, too. What else was there to do? The queen herself rounded her desk and also reclaimed her seat.

They were all quiet. Ember could see Eli struggling to come up with something to say in the strained silence, but it didn't seem like cracking that silence ought to be their place.

And it only lasted long enough to make it clear that they were, no matter what sort of friendliness the queen projected, at her mercy. She even controlled how strained and awkward the moments of silence in the room were.

"As I was saying," she began after that too-long moment, "I believe I've found useful employment for you both. But first, a few preliminaries. How long are you planning to stay in Frost?"

Ember glanced at Eli again, uncertain of the answer. This trip had been his idea, but they'd never talked about what would happen once they found the city. Given that neither of them had been truly certain that Frost even existed, talking about what they would do once they got there seemed almost irrelevant.

But it suddenly no longer seemed irrelevant. Frost was real, and they were inside it, now in an audience with the queen. What were they planning to do now?

Eli pulled in a breath, long and slow as he thought through his next words. "Well," he said, his eyes flashing to Ember as though to confirm the truth of his words, "we're not really sure."

"So you have no plans to return to Dusk?"

"No. No plans to."

"Hmm. And what do you want to be doing now that you're here?"

These were the sorts of questions Ember had expected to come up when they first got into the city. Questions of their plans, their intentions, what they expected to find once they'd come through the wall. To have these questions so delayed was almost disorienting.

Eli didn't answer. Ember couldn't help him; she didn't have any answers to the question either.

The queen picked up a couple of papers and tapped their bottoms against her desk until they all lined up in a neat little pile. "So, let me see if I understand correctly. You traveled across the tundra for days — I know Dusk is many days away on foot — braving Our Mother knows what sort of weather and monsters like my city only has nightmares about, and never once did you stop to consider what you would do once you reached my walls? Is that about right?"

Eli's head drooped under the sharpness that had entered her tone.

"No," Ember cut in.

The queen lifted her eyebrows, pulling the blue of her eyelids up so it became visible over her dark eyelashes. "No?"

"The truth is, we weren't even sure this place was real. We didn't exactly talk about what we wanted to do once we reached it, but that was only because we were so focused on actually reaching it. And … there were no monsters."

"None at all?"

Ember shook her head.

"Well." The queen smiled. "Mother Atalanta smiled kindly on your travels."

"Mmm." It wasn't agreement, but Ember hoped it wouldn't sound like disagreement, either. Eli had buried almost a tenth of their food for the trip into the snow before eating in the hopes that Atalanta would grant them safe passage. Ember wasn't sure if those sacrifices had been worth it. True, they'd made it safely, but it wasn't like anyone had smiled down on them during their travel. The weather had been brutal, especially in the final three days.

"Since you have no plans to leave, I might as well tell you about the work I've found. Perhaps once you are contributing members of my city, you'll feel less inclined to be unsure of how much we value your presence." She tapped another handful of papers into a neat pile and set them to one side of her desk, then fixed Ember with a long, appreciative look. "I hear you're good with machines."

Something sparked in Ember's thoughts, some small buried hope that she'd had when first seeing the force field and the electric lights of the city. She'd hoped she'd be able to get a glimpse of the machines that made such things possible, a hope that had been extinguished by the strange reaction Felix had when she asked him about the electricity. But now she felt her spine straightening and her expression brightening despite herself.

She kept her response even and careful, however. The last thing she wanted was for the queen to know how much she wanted to see Frost's machines. "I've been tinkering most of my life."

"She's being modest," Eli added. "She's very good with machines. She has a knack for understanding how things work."

The queen smiled. "As you might expect of a scientist's daughter."

Ember blinked, startled by the words. It was an offhanded comment, not meant to be read into. But Ember couldn't remember if she'd ever mentioned to anyone in Frost that her father had been a scientist. In fact, she had a very distinct memory of *not* saying that very thing when Maudie first asked if there was anything she was good at. Because she was pretty sure Maudie had asked her if she was a scientist, and she'd said no, she wasn't, for the reason that she didn't really want to think about her father in front of the over-friendly Frost stranger.

"How…?" she started to ask, but then swallowed the rest of the question before she'd made enough noise to bring the queen's attention all the way back to her.

Maybe Eli had said something while she was out yesterday. It wasn't like her father was some kind of secret — the fact that she didn't want to talk about him had more to do with the pain her memories brought her than because she was embarrassed or ashamed of his profession.

And the queen didn't seem interested in pursuing that particular conversation — it had been a nothing statement. But it left Ember feeling uneasy, uncertain of what else the queen might know that hadn't been told to her. She tried to remind herself that she hadn't done anything wrong, except maybe leaving the apartment yesterday, and she'd only done that because no one had bothered to stop her.

"I was so glad to hear it," the queen was saying now. "I'm in desperate need of some help. My Envoys have reported some strange malfunctions with my dolls, and I need a scientist to work on them."

"I'm not a scientist. Not really. I just tinker."

The queen's expression fell. Ember could feel Eli's eyes boring into her temple. Judging her.

Maybe, just this once, it might behoove her to be nice.

"But … I can take a look anyway."

The queen folded her hands. Her fingers, like her face, were so pale that the network of blue veins under her skin was visible. Her nails were blue. For a moment, Ember wondered if she was in danger of losing her fingers to the cold, but then noticed the faint sparkle in the blue fingernails. She'd painted them that color, probably to match her lips and eyelids. "Well, I would expect nothing less from the daughter of Mikail Dominikovich."

Chapter Twelve

How DID the queen of Frost know the name of Ember's father?

Ember's thoughts wouldn't stop turning, and all of them refused to make any sort of sense. The queen's attention had turned to Eli, and from the sound of it, the conversation had lost some of the urgency Ember had picked up from the queen. Still, even when she tried to listen to what they were saying, she couldn't understand more than a few words at a time.

"... Excellent for ... and such a remarkable ... much obliged..."

She wished they would either speak loud enough to cut through her churning mind, or they would be quiet and let her think. This in-between neither-nor was extremely annoying.

A few minutes of conversation with Eli, and then the queen was standing and motioning them to do the same. She took their hands one at a time again, first Eli's, then Ember's, squeezing them gently between both of her own hands. "It's been such a pleasure, my friends," she said once she'd dropped Ember's hand. "I'll send for you in the morning."

"Goddene, ma'am," Eli answered in his most respectful tone.

Ember didn't say anything. She couldn't with all the questions clogging up her mind and throat.

Maudie, who must've been waiting, and maybe even listening, at the door, came in as though those words were her cue. The queen nodded at Maudie, and then Maudie led them out of the room, down the hallway, and through the front doors of the palace.

Ember let out a breath as the front doors closed and she took her first step onto the slick glass bridge. Somehow, the bridge felt like the least treacherous thing she'd had to navigate so far, and judging by the relief that crossed Eli's face, he felt similarly.

"How did it go?" Maudie asked, and for a moment, her smile seemed almost genuine. A flash of real curiosity beneath her usually off-putting, manufactured manner.

"Good, I think," Eli said, and Ember didn't bother to contradict it. "She's..." He hesitated, took a couple of steps on the bridge, watching his feet to keep from fumbling. "Nice?"

"Oh, yes. The most kind and generous queen we could ever hope for. It's thanks to her that we have all we do."

Maybe it was just that Ember knew Eli so well that she'd heard the way his voice turned up at the end, making what should've been a statement into a question. Maybe Maudie just didn't know how to pick up on those sorts of subtleties. It would hardly be the most surprising thing about the Frost woman.

Ember had never felt more grateful for solid ground beneath her feet. The last of the tightness that had gripped her shoulders and back since she woke up this morning eased as they made it safely off the bridge and back into the palace square.

A voice called her name. She turned and saw Felix jogging toward her, grinning bright enough to rival the sunlight streaming into the square. He slowed when Eli turned toward him, too. "Sorry," he said, glancing at Eli like he'd just realized he was interrupting. "Is this not a good time?"

"It's fine," Ember answered before Eli could say otherwise. "We're just coming from the queen."

A bit of that brightness returned to Felix's face. "That's right. How is she?"

"Good?" She didn't mean for her word to tilt up at the end like she wasn't sure of her answer. She coughed and tried again. "She has work for us."

Felix smiled in response, apparently either fooled or willing to pretend he was fooled.

Eli cleared his throat, a pointed noise that made Ember recall that he hadn't been with her yesterday when she met Felix — and, she remembered, she hadn't told him about her new Frost friend, either. "Eli, this is Felix. Felix, my friend Eli."

Felix held out his hand just like the queen had. "Also from Dusk?"

Eli accepted it, but he wasn't smiling. "Of course."

"A pleasure."

"Mm." He dropped Felix's hand.

"Felix showed me around town a bit yesterday," Ember said into the moment of awkward silence that settled over them.

Eli lifted an eyebrow. "You didn't tell me you'd made a friend."

"You didn't ask." She would've said something about Felix if Eli had asked — but he hadn't, so she didn't. She still wasn't sure why she'd chosen not to volunteer it and didn't want to think about it anyway.

"What are you doing here?" she asked, turning away from Eli and his annoyed little frown.

Felix shrugged. His face was shifting toward red. "Honestly? I was hoping to see you."

Ember swallowed. There was a lump in her throat, but she wasn't sure where it had come from or what it was doing there.

"But I didn't mean to interrupt," he added hastily. "If you have somewhere else you need to be…" He glanced at Maudie as if the question were for her.

Maudie smiled. "There is nothing else for now." She bobbed her head to Ember and Eli and backed away. "You are free to do as you please."

Felix grinned and turned back to Ember. "Do you want to do something?"

Ember glanced at Eli, who was still frowning slightly as though unsure of what to make of her Frost friend. Felix followed her gaze and redoubled his smile. "Either of you," he added, trying, and mostly succeeding, at sounding like that was what he meant the whole time, that he hadn't totally forgotten that Eli was there. "I took Ember around a bit last night, but I'd be happy to show you, too."

Eli shrugged. "Whatever you want."

"You mentioned something about moving pictures?"

Felix's face brightened. "Oh, you wanna see one?"

"Can we?"

"Yeah. The theater's this way." He gestured for them to follow, and Ember stepped eagerly forward, but Eli caught her arm and stilled her feet.

"What are you doing?" he hissed.

Ember frowned. "Going to find out what a moving picture is?"

"By following a stranger into an unfamiliar city."

Oh. That was what Eli's scowling was about — not the chance to look around Frost, but Felix himself. She smiled and hoped she looked reassuring. "You don't have to worry about Felix. He's a nice boy."

"How do you know that?"

"Because I've already met him."

"And so you know you can trust him?"

Ember sighed. For the first time, Eli was having some kind of healthy suspicion, but it had to be about Felix?

"Coming?" Felix asked over his shoulder.

"Yes," Ember answered, glaring at Eli as she pulled away from his grip. "We are."

ELI CONTINUED to shoot Felix weird looks all the way down to the theater and then still after Felix bought them tickets and they settled into a dark room full of soft, upholstered chairs.

Ember mostly ignored him. He'd picked a strange time to switch on the worst of his skepticism, but that was his own problem, not hers, and she kept up a light stream of conversation with Felix instead as they waited for the moving picture to begin.

"What is this?" she asked, keeping her voice down as seemed appropriate for the room but unable to stop her fingers from stroking the upholstery on the chair. She'd never felt anything so soft and luxurious and wonderful.

Felix glanced down to see what she was asking about and grinned. "Velvet, or something like it, anyway. Probably from the garment district."

Ember remembered the trolley ride yesterday, how fast it moved and how she'd seen only the square and the old city. And now there was a garment district? And fields to the east where they grew their food? It seemed impossible. "How big is Frost?"

"Well, it stretches from the north wall to the south, and then from the Eastern to the Western Sea. There aren't even trolleys that go all the way out to its edges."

Ember marveled. She didn't know what that all meant — she had no idea what the Eastern or Western Sea were — but the idea that a trolley couldn't cover all the distance was remarkable anyway.

And the marvels weren't over. At that moment, the moving picture began, and for the next hour, Ember couldn't say anything at all.

She'd seen pictures before, in the couple of books that had survived the years, and even one framed in wood that Korrah had showed her of someplace she claimed to have gone to once, with metal buildings even taller than the ones in Frost. Taking what she knew about pictures and trying to imagine them moving so they became a moving picture was something she could kind of wrap her head around.

But her imagining couldn't prepare her for what she saw. Because it wasn't just a single picture that moved, but an entire sequence of pictures so she was following a character through an adventure. It wasn't just a picture — it was a story. A fictional one, obviously, since the characters rode around on these big, four-legged, hairy animals that moved faster than trolleys through strange, unfrozen lands full of trees, but still a story.

As the moving picture ended, Ember remained still, gaping at the now-blank screen in the front of the room even as the lights came back on and the other people started to talk and get up from their velvet seats.

Felix glanced over at her, and his smile could've lit up the room all on its own with how big and bright it got. "Like it?" he ventured at last.

"I ... don't even know what to say. That was..."

Words failed her. She let them dribble into silence.

"Interesting?" Eli offered from her other side.

Ember shot him a look. "Interesting doesn't even begin to cover it. It was like there really were people here. Like, like a play, but better. More. How do they do it?"

"The queen likes moving pictures."

Which wasn't an answer, but Ember decided not to push, worried about toggling that switch inside him that would turn off his answers completely.

Felix stood. "I'm glad you enjoyed it."

Ember and Eli followed him out of the room, Ember's thoughts still spinning with how the moving pictures could work. Maybe, if there was a machine that flashed a lot of still pictures really, really fast, that could do it. But then how could someone capture that many still pictures? Was there someone inside the walls of Frost who just drew hundreds, thousands, maybe more, pictures to feed into a machine that ran them really fast? Was that even possible? The people had seemed so real, like they were actually in the room, even though there was no way they could be, not on their animals and shooting their guns.

They left the theater and meandered down the street with no special purpose. Eli's sudden grumpiness had been soothed by the excitement of the moving picture, and now he and Felix were talking with increasing ease, allowing Ember's thoughts to drift.

Maybe it was all just starting to sink in now: the fact that they'd left Dusk, found Frost. That it was somehow even more incredible than the stories had always said. It didn't seem possible, and yet, here she was, walking down a street full of sunlight — albeit weak winter sunlight — where there was no snow on the ground and her exposed arms and legs hadn't turned black and fallen off in the cold. Stepping out of a darkened theater where pictures moved and people rode strange hairy beasts and strangers gave away food just to be friendly.

Everything else, the strange way the queen addressed her, the ominous sound of the I'll-send-for-you-tomorrow, the dropping of her father's name amongst everything — that was all behind her. Ember liked Frost, even if she didn't like its queen, and now everything would be all right.

Chapter Thirteen

Maudie came for Ember before sunrise the next morning and brought her back to the palace, but not to the queen's room like yesterday, instead leading her through hallways that looked pretty much identical to the ones she'd seen before around the palace, and only Ember's decent sense of direction told her that she wasn't actually just walking the same route as she had before.

After a few turns, Maudie waved her into a busy room off the busy hallway and up to a red-haired man in a brilliant white suit and the shiniest, blackest shoes Ember had ever seen. He looked Ember up and down, then glanced at a paper he held clipped to a thin wooden board. "You must be our new guest," he said, to the board rather than her. "Yes, the queen did mention you'd be coming."

Ember didn't answer.

"Come with me," he said, finally looked up from his board. "The queen has some dolls that need fixing. They've started spitting nonsense and had to be taken out of rotation."

"Dolls?"

"This way." The man gestured for Ember to follow him. She did, slowly, wondering what she was in for. All the dolls she'd ever known about were ones made of scrap bits of cloth, maybe with button eyes or stuffing if there were scraps of either to spare. The fanciest one was an heirloom porcelain doll owned by Grieg's family, and mostly his daughter brought it out to show off, because Masha Grieganova was that sort of obnoxious.

They didn't go far, turning off the hallway into a mostly empty room as nondescript and functional as the one they'd just come from, without the grandeur of the queen's end of the palace and not at all the machine room of yesterday. There was a table of sturdy wood at one end, and it was covered with what appeared to be every sort of tool a person could ever need. Two people sat at the other end of the room, smiling widely at nothing.

Ember ignored them, though she could feel their eyes on her — she doubted she would ever not sense those unnerving Frost smiles against her skin whenever she was in the presence of them. But the table of tools was far more interesting to her, and the redheaded man didn't stop her from wandering over to look at them a little more closely, so she figured that was allowed.

They were a glorious assortment. Pliers of every imaginable shape and size. Wrenches and solder. Wire-cutters and magnifying glasses and little lights that didn't even seem to draw from whatever electrical sources that powered the rest of the city. Ember ran her fingers over the tools with the reverence a worshiper might across the bottom of an Atalanta statue.

"Are these for me? To use?" she breathed at last when the man came up behind her.

"If they aren't sufficient, you need only ask for more,"

the man answered. "The queen will have it made. What-ever you need."

Ember blinked up at him, startled for a moment at the idea of *not* finding this bounty sufficient. As if there was anything *more* that she could need.

He didn't respond to her surprise, only turned toward the people sitting at the other end of the room and nodding. "Well, then."

The words sounded like a summons, or an order, but Ember wasn't sure what of. Perhaps to the people watching her, though neither of them moved at his comment. She waited silently, ready to have a look at the dolls she was here to fix, and for a moment, the room was still.

Then the redheaded man turned back to her, eyebrows raised, lips pressing into a frown. "Go on, then."

Ember hesitated. Other than the table full of tools and the two other people, there was nothing in the room. She didn't think she was missing the dolls, and another scan of the space confirmed that for her. "Go on what?" she ventured at last.

The man's lips quirked again, this time with definite annoyance. "The dolls, *devushka*."

"Yes. Where…?"

The question died on her lips as she realized what she'd missed before. As it sunk in what exactly she was looking at. She pulled in a too-sharp breath and looked over at the people sitting in the room across from her.

No, not people. *Dolls.*

Something like fear, or maybe even panic, lanced through her body, splintering like ice into her veins, as she looked back at the dolls, their unnervingly wide smiles and fixed stares. She'd seen those expressions before on many of the people around Frost: the trolley drivers and strangers in the streets. Maudie.

Were *all* of them dolls? Mechanical people, programming to look and behave like people, except for those unwavering smiles? Ember's hands shook at the idea, and she reached blindly for something on the table to hold in order to keep that fact concealed.

She ended up with a pair of little needle-nose pliers. Which was probably as good a tool as any to start with.

But start with what?

She took a couple of steps toward the dolls. They watched her curiously, smiling and still. "Um. Are you malfunctioning?"

One, the man — could dolls be men? Women? People at all? What should she call them in her own head and out in the world? — met her gaze, and somehow, impossibly, his smile widened, exposing teeth as bright white as fresh snow in sunlight. He stood up and came toward her, and she was suddenly reminded of her first venture into the city, the man — the doll? — who'd approached her while she and Felix were waiting for the trolley to take them to the old city, the way he'd bared down on her just like this.

Ember clenched her pliers tight in her fingers. It wasn't a knife, but just having *something* in her hands made her feel infinitely more prepared for whatever this doll might do.

But would a knife, or pliers, or weapons of any kind, do anything against a mechanical person? Could they be cut? Hurt? Killed?

She flinched away, from both the doll and the thought.

The doll paused, just a little too close to her face for comfort. His smile never wavered. "The wall is cracking."

EMBER HAD NEVER CONSIDERED what made a person. That was the sort of question that wouldn't have made sense to her before — if it looked and walked and talked like a person, then it was one, wasn't it?

She was wondering now.

She stared down at the doll, crumpled gracelessly at her feet, its eyes staring as open and vacant as a corpse, and she had to swallow hard against the bile rising in her throat.

The red-haired man had finally elected to take the chair the doll had vacated and have a seat a few paces away from where Ember worked. He got up again as the doll fell, expression alarmed. "What did you—"

"I don't know," Ember interrupted. Cold sweat beaded at her hairline, and her stomach flopped over. "I just..." She couldn't finish the sentence. What was the end of it?

Killed someone?

The other doll, the female-looking one, turned to Ember, and for the first time, her smile faltered.

It was that, probably more than anything, that left her wondering. She'd been mucking around in the first doll's head, beneath a layer of hair and manufactured skin and a thin metal panel that popped open beneath her fingertips, for at least an hour, and mostly she'd been able to keep her fingers from shaking, her thoughts from wandering.

But now...

She hadn't meant to drop the doll to the floor. She didn't know what she was doing with all the blinking bits of electrics inside the doll's head — gears and belts and joints, she understood, but not electrics. Not lights and programming.

But Vallenovich would hear none of her attempts to explain that to him. Apparently, the queen had told him that Ember was the girl who would be fixing their dolls, and nothing Ember herself said would deter him.

So Ember fiddled away with the inside of the doll's

blinking head, and now he — it — was lying at her feet, as blank and unresponsive as a dead body.

Vallenovich looked over the doll again, a small frown on his pressed-thin lips. He crouched for a moment to be nearer to eye-level with the unresponsive body, stared at it, considered before standing back up and turning his attention to Ember again. "Well. It's not exactly what I had in mind, but perhaps it'll do for now."

Ember's stomach flopped again. Her saliva turned sour and warm, and she swallowed, hard and fast, until the queasiness eased.

Vallenovich nodded toward the female doll. "Go on, then."

Ember glanced at the doll; it looked back at her, not smiling, and the loss of that single doll-like expression turned her face so utterly human that this time bile actually rose into Ember's mouth.

She clamped her teeth together, jammed her hand against her mouth, and swallowed down the sensation, nearly gagging at the taste as the vomit nearly touched her tongue.

Slowly, slowly, the trembling in her limbs quieted, and the nausea passed again. Ember lowered her hand — the other one was fisted hard around the pliers — and took a step toward the doll.

It didn't move, barely reacted at all, only stared at her until it couldn't keep her in its sights without turning. Ember nudged aside its hair, opened the panel of skin and metal at the back of its head, and stared down into another head of blinking lights and tiny wires.

I'm sorry, she thought, though she didn't dare open her mouth to say it. *I'm sorry, I'm sorry, I'm sorry...*

She touched the pliers to the place in the doll's head

that had dropped the first one, and the female doll slumped like the dead over its chair.

THE QUEEN WAS WAITING in the big room when the redheaded man took Ember back to it after finishing with the dolls.

He startled and then bowed low to her. "Your Highness," he gasped at the deepest part of his bow. "To what do I owe the honor of your presence?"

The queen made a funny sort of waving gesture at him, a clear dismissal. "Never mind the formalities, Vallenovich — I only wanted to see how our new mechanic did on her first assignment."

The queen looked from the red-haired man — Vallenovich — to Ember, one eyebrow raised. If she had hair there like a normal person, Ember imagined it would be arched, as dramatic as the rest of her face. "Turned them off?"

"I wasn't sure what else to do." Ember didn't mean for her voice to come out sounding so uncertain, but the twisting anxiety of the day hadn't yet left her stomach. The blank, staring eyes of the dolls would surely haunt her dreams tonight.

Vallenovich hadn't raised himself from his bow. His voice was muffled by the way it was directed at the floor. "She says there's nothing wrong with them."

"There isn't," Ember cut in.

The queen turned all her attention onto Ember then. Ember fought against the urge to flinch under her gaze. "Nothing wrong?"

"Not anything obvious, anyway. Nothing I could find."

The queen just stared, that same hairless eyebrow raised in continued question.

Ember changed the subject, hoping that she could maybe get an answer from the queen. After all, if the queen didn't know what the dolls might mean, who would? "They're saying the wall is cracking."

The queen went very still at the words. She hadn't moved much before, of course, but there was a different kind of stillness to her now. She was suddenly a statue made of rock and ice, those strange dark eyes boring into Ember like she wanted to tap directly into her very thoughts.

Ember forced herself to meet the queen's gaze. She hadn't done anything wrong, so there was no reason to hide from her.

"Say that again," the queen said slowly, each word coming like it was being punched from her throat.

"The dolls. They're saying the wall is cracking."

The queen pushed suddenly past Vallenovich, who was at last coming out of his bow at Ember's words, darting forward and snatching Ember's arm in a grip that hurt. "Is that what's happening? All my dolls that have been malfunctioning? They're telling people that the wall is cracking?"

"I…" Ember's voice caught and shredded against the lump rising in her throat. She swallowed hard and forced her words to stay level. "I don't know. It's what the dolls I saw today were saying."

And the ones she'd seen out on the streets, the ones that had been taken away by people in white suits and shiny black shoes like Vallenovich's, but she didn't add that part.

"They can't be doing that. Do you understand me?" The queen's fingers shook, and her grip was so tight Ember could already feel the bruises beginning to form beneath their pressure. "Under no circumstances can the dolls be saying such things. Do you understand?"

"I … no, not really. Why's the wall cracking?"

The queen brought her face very close to Ember's, and the sudden closeness stopped the question dead on Ember's tongue. No warmth leaked off her skin — even her breath smelled like ice. Just another thing about her to confuse and frighten Ember. Even the dolls emitted heat, radiating it off their skin surfaces like a normal person. She met Ember's eyes with a ferocity of someone trying to communicate much more with their expression than what they were saying with their words, but what she was trying to say, Ember didn't understand.

"Listen to me, Ember Mikailanova. Listen to me very closely. The wall is not cracking. The dolls are speaking lies."

Chapter Fourteen

EMBER HAD NEVER BEEN MORE grateful to leave a place as she was to get out of the palace that day, but she couldn't stop staring at Maudie as the other woman — the doll — took her back to her room. There was a strange new tension in her escort's expression, though perhaps that was only Ember projecting anxiety onto a mechanical being that couldn't actually feel anything at all.

Eli was sitting on the couch when she came into the room, but he got right to his feet when Ember came in as if able to sense her distress.

He'd always been good at that.

He took Ember's hand, gently, and tugged her, just as gently, over to the couch. Sat and urged her to do the same. "Tell me."

Maudie was gone. Ember and Eli were alone.

Maybe she ought to tell him. Maybe it would help.

Maudie. The trolley drivers. So many of the people they'd passed on the streets. Even the woman who'd sold them the tickets to the moving picture.

Dolls. All of them. Smiling too wide and performing

duties that must not be of much interest to the people of Frost.

How many of them were dolls? How many people did Frost actually have?

Did the actual people, the flesh-and-blood ones, know? Did they even care?

Ember had always felt watched in Frost — even if that feeling was based more on how she thought she ought to feel rather than what was actually happening around her — and now she knew why.

Because half, or maybe more, of the people she met were mechanical people, programmed with those unnerving smiles, tasked with doing who-knew-what in the city.

Were there dolls nearby? How good was their hearing? Could she whisper quiet enough to not be overheard? Would it even matter?

"Ember." Eli squeezed the hand he still held, pulling her attention back to him. "What is it?"

"Nothing," Ember answered automatically, then paused to reconsider the truth of that statement. "It's … maybe nothing."

"You don't think it's nothing. Just tell me."

"The people here. The smiling ones like Maudie. They're not people."

This was definitely not what Eli had expected her to say — both his eyebrows went all the way up at the words. "Not people?" he repeated slowly, turning the words over in his mouth as if he didn't know what they meant.

"I mean, maybe they are people, I don't know. What makes a person a person?"

"What kind of question is that?"

"The one I've been thinking about all day."

Eli snorted. "Since when have you been philosophical?"

"Since I turned off two maybe-people today."

"Ember. You're not making sense."

"The people, or ... or not-people. They call them dolls. They're mechanical, and some of them are saying things."

"Mechanical people?" Again, he repeated the words like he didn't understand them. Like the very words themselves didn't make any sense.

Which was fair, Ember thought. She'd struggled to understand them herself all day, and so far, she wasn't sure she'd gotten any closer to it than she was the first time they tangled in her head.

"Dolls. The smiling ones. Maudie, the trolley driver, almost half of the people riding inside of them. All of them — they're mechanical. I think it's like half the population of Frost, from what I've seen on the streets."

Eli frowned, but he wasn't really listening to her. "That's not possible."

"I wouldn't have thought so, either, but then I saw them. The insides of them. It's all circuitry. You can turn them off if you touch the right part in the back of their heads. I did it. Twice. And I think the queen will be having me do it again and again, because the dolls — they're saying things."

"Wait. No. Stop it." Eli's attention snapped back to her all at once, and the sudden force of it stilled Ember's tongue. "I know where you're going with this, and I'm not interested."

"I'm not 'going' anywhere."

"Yes, you are. You wanna drag me into some kind of conspiracy theory of yours, and I'm not going there."

"That's not—"

"Don't. We both know I'm right. I'm. Not. Interested." He turned each of the last words into their own sentence.

Ember hadn't flinched under the queen's gaze. She hadn't even when the queen dug her fingers into her arm tight enough to bruise. She'd looked straight at the queen's unnerving dark eyes and waited for her to say what she needed to say, recognizing by the force of it that she was lying, to herself or to Ember, or maybe to both, but lying just the same.

Ember flinched now.

Eli softened a little at that, one hand shifting toward her as if to reach for her hand or arm. He hesitated before actually completing the gesture and let his arm fall awkwardly against his leg instead. "Not everything is a mystery you need to solve. Some things are none of your business, and you shouldn't go poking your nose into things that aren't."

"This isn't one of those things."

"Are you sure? Really, truly certain? Because you know that once you start, you'll never stop."

"Eli—"

"Ember," he echoed back in the same half-frustrated tone. "Stay out of it. Not everything is a mystery you have to solve."

Chapter Fifteen

ELI'S WORDS echoed in her head as she went to bed, tried to sleep, as she eventually gave up and made her way back out of the room, through the electrically lit streets and to the palace square.

She found herself drawn to the Atalanta statue, which glimmered in the electric lights of the night. She sat cross-legged in front of it and stared up at the statue's face, triumphant over the dead beast at her feet.

None of her business, indeed. The queen had seemed quite pleased to *make* it her business — it was her, after all, who assigned her to the dolls and then reacted so strongly to the words they repeated.

Eli was wrong. There was something strange going on in Frost, something that the queen was determined to hide, and she was putting Ember smack in the middle of it whether she intended to or not.

The people — the dolls — knew her name. Her patronymic. They knew her, and they kept trying to tell her that the wall was cracking, whatever that was supposed to mean. That made it her business. Her mystery to solve.

She couldn't remember the last time she'd prayed. Frankly, prayer was an activity she mostly left to Eli and his mother — she knew they prayed over her enough that she shouldn't need to say anything on her own behalf.

But, today, she found herself praying. For the strength to carry on, for something to finally make some kind of sense she could follow. For the discernment to tell the difference between truth and lies.

Because she was beginning to suspect that a lot of what she was being told were indeed lies. And a lot of those lies seemed to be centered on the queen herself.

Ember might've dozed out there in front of the Atalanta statue. The next thing she really knew about her surroundings was a warm hand suddenly touching her shoulder.

She leapt to her feet, knocking off the hand, and spun to face the person, but relaxed when she recognized him. "Felix." His name punched out of her like a sigh.

Felix smiled that cheerful grin of his, but he shifted his weight from foot to foot as if uncomfortable, and he kept his voice down like he didn't want to disturb anyone else. "Godden, Ember."

"Is it morning already?" she mumbled, mostly to herself.

He grinned again, but his ears were tinging pink. The color clashed with his hair so badly it was almost adorable. "It'll do that. Time, I mean. Moves on."

He wasn't here to tell her about how time worked. Ember smiled acknowledgment and waited.

"Are you hungry? Have you had breakfast?"

Ah, there it was. He wanted to offer her breakfast. What was it about this Frost boy and feeding her?

Not that she was complaining. Breakfast with Felix sounded like fun.

In Dusk, for a man to offer a woman food was a statement. Maybe not of official intentions, exactly, but of the fact that those intentions were crossing the man's mind.

Those apples during their first conversation couldn't have been that; that time, he was just being nice. Sharing the bounty that Frost apparently had.

This time, though, it felt like a statement. One that Ember found herself wanting to return.

And — the thought jumped suddenly into her mind — perhaps he would be someone who could tell her about the wall, and what it meant that it was cracking.

"I haven't had breakfast," she answered. Then, because she wondered what it would feel like, what sort of reaction it would provoke, she let a little cheek slip into her smile. Just a touch, she hoped, not too much to make it obvious. "Do you wanna take me?"

The pink in his ears spilled onto his cheeks. The dusting of freckles over the bridge of his nose stood out like stars in the darkened sky. "I ... yeah. If you want."

"I do want. Very much."

A fresh grin, lodged halfway between pleased and relieved, spread across his face. "Have you been to the Queen's Cross Café yet?"

Ember shook her head.

"Well, let's go."

The Queen's Cross Café was a few blocks beyond the square, marked by a wooden sign over the door. Felix opened the door and held it open for her. Warmth like the heat from a roaring fire poured out through the door; it carried with it some of the unfamiliar food scents Ember had occasionally caught on the edges of the Frost breeze.

She stepped through the door, and Felix followed her, letting the door shut on its own behind him. The room was large and square, lit with several electric bulbs hanging in glass domes from the ceiling. A dozen or more square wooden tables were scattered neatly about the room; a couple of people sat around one of the tables, sipping from large porcelain teacups.

A woman wearing a dark apron over her white Frost dress came out through a doorway to the right, perhaps alerted by the little bell that tinkled over the door when Felix let it close. "Godden," she said with an unnaturally wide smile.

A doll. Ember smiled and forced it to hold a little brightness. The doll didn't seem to notice her especially, its mechanical eyes skipping over to Felix as if familiar or comfortable with him. "Table for two?"

"Yes, please," Felix answered.

The doll grabbed a couple of papers from the small stack on the nearby table and gestured for them to follow. It led them to one of the tables away from the other occupied one, close to the glass walls that covered half the room.

Felix sat, then grinned when Ember hesitated. She lifted her chin just a little in an effort to prove that she wasn't confused or intimidated, and sat, too. The doll handed each of them a sheet of paper, which Ember saw was printed with several food and beverage options, then smiled and said it'd give them a minute to look over the menu.

"Order whatever you want," Felix said. "This is my treat."

Ember watched the doll walk away, its hips swinging beneath its Frost-woman clothing as if it was feeling saucy and wanted people in the cafe to notice it. Such a small thing, a little human affectation, and it made Ember's stomach twist.

"Ember?" Felix frowned at her, concerned. "You okay?"

"Oh. Yeah, sorry." Her words tumbled past her lips like lies, so she smiled briefly at him and turned her attention back to the menu to prove she was fine.

Almost nothing on the paper sounded even a little bit familiar. Rice and cafei, she knew, but she'd never heard of eggs, sausage, or muffins, hot chocolate or au laits.

She set down the menu and glanced over at Felix, who was grinning again, apparently amused by whatever expression had leaked onto Ember's face. "Hot chocolate and an egg," he said before she could ask. "That's my favorite."

When the doll in the black apron came back and asked them what they wanted, Ember asked for hot chocolate and an egg.

"Whipped cream?" the doll said.

Ember didn't have a chance to look confused or ask her what she meant before Felix answered for her. "Yes."

He asked for a sausage muffin and a cafei, then went back to grinning happily at Ember when the doll bustled off, menus in its hand again. "You don't know what apples or eggs or hot chocolate are — what do you eat up there?"

Had someone else asked the question, she might've been offended. But Felix was so sincere, so innocently curious, that she didn't even mind answering. "Rice. Tea. Every week, we get a ration of jerky. Once in a great while, we'll get a bit of cafei. I'd been saving that up for a special occasion."

She fought against the urge to blush at the admission. Hoarding rations was as close to a crime as was possible to get in Dusk, and she hadn't told anyone but Eli that she was doing it for fear of being attacked in the streets.

Surely such a thing wasn't a terrible thing to admit

here in Frost, where rationing didn't even seem to be a practice. Why should it be? Frost grew its own food.

Felix was quiet for a single beat after she finished, as though waiting for her to go on and continue listing the sorts of food people ate in Dusk. "Is that all?" he prompted when he seemed to realize that Ember wasn't about to go on.

Again, a sort of question that might infuriate her had it not been Felix who was asking it. "Yes. Rice, tea, jerky. All of it was stored away Before and has been running out ever since."

Another flush of heat crept across her face, and again, she tried to breathe slowly in and out to cool it. Everyone in Dusk knew that the rations were running out — portions had gotten smaller, and sometimes they went as many as ten days between one jerky ration and the next. The council was trying to spread out the decreasing stores thinner so they would last longer. But, like hoarding rations, mentioning the fact that they were running low was about as close to a crime as was possible to commit.

Everyone knew it, and everyone was in denial.

"You're running out of food?" Felix asked, interrupting Ember's thoughts.

She couldn't meet his eyes; she nodded toward the wooden table instead.

"Is that why you came here?"

It would be simple to say yes, to let him think that was the main reason that had motivated her to leave Dusk. It was such a simple, obvious answer. But it wasn't the truth, or at least not all of it. And she found that she wanted to tell Felix the truth, at least as best as she could.

"I came because Eli was going, and nothing I could say would make him stay. There was nothing there for either of us, and if I hadn't come with him, then there would've really been nothing there for me." She was aware even as she said it that she was jumbling her words, tripping over what should've been a simple sort of explanation. "Does that make sense?"

Felix nodded. The grin was gone from his face; his expression had turned serious. "He's your ... boyfriend? Husband?"

"Eli?" She chuckled. "Oh, no. He's been like my brother my entire life, and I love him dearly, but there's nothing romantic between us."

Felix lifted an eyebrow. "You sure about that?"

"Yes," she said firmly. "Everyone in Dusk expected us to get married, but..." She shuddered, exaggerating it a bit so there would be no question in his mind what she thought of the idea.

That Eli himself had mentioned it, once, at the start of the summer, just before his desire to find Frost went from a dream to an obsession, she didn't want to admit, and certainly not to Felix.

"So you're unattached?" He asked like the words tasted bad coming out, but they were words that he needed an answer to.

She must've not been as clear as she'd hoped. She tried again. "Yes."

Felix reached out, a little hesitantly, and rested his fingers on Ember's. "I'm glad to hear it," he said. His eyes kept flickering down toward the table, his voice quiet and uncertain, as though he wasn't sure if this was something he was allowed to say.

Ember looked down at their hands, just barely touching each other in the space the table had set between them. No boy had ever touched her like that, soft, hesitant, like he was ready to take his hand back at the slightest twitch that might indicate she didn't like it.

But she didn't want to twitch away, although something somewhere inside her more suspicious self was telling her maybe she should. After all, she didn't really know Felix. For all that he seemed genuine and kind, he could be hiding any number of worrisome motives. He could be a spy for the queen or an assassin sent to get close to her before sticking a knife in her belly and harvesting her for meat.

Ember dismissed all those thoughts, turned her hand over, and closed her fingers around his.

There was beat of silence, a strained sort of uncertainty between them. Ember didn't dare look up, even when she could feel Felix watching her, for fear that the heat in her face would give her away; she kept her eyes stubbornly on their hands. She liked the way they looked like that, her Dusk-dark skin against his Frost-pale, the way it felt for someone to touch her like that, soft, hesitant, uncertain, but obviously wanting.

She'd never been *wanted* before.

The doll in the apron came back to the table at that moment, balancing two plates and two large porcelain cups in its hands, and both Ember and Felix jerked away from each other as if they'd nearly been caught doing something wrong. Ember could light a fire with the heat in her face.

But the doll didn't seem to notice, or maybe just didn't care — it smiled and set down a plate and cup in front of each of them without comment. "Enjoy," it chirped, "and don't hesitate to ask if you need anything."

Ember stared down at her plate, at the strange semi-solid puddle of what she assumed was eggs — thin whitish skin, slightly burned at the very edges, surrounding a bright yellow centers. The cup was full to overflowing, a small trickle of thick brown liquid spilling out from underneath a swirling pile of white.

Felix was grinning again. "Try it," he urged.

She stuck her finger experimentally into the pile above the lip of the cup. The stuff was so foamy and light that even when she scooped some onto her finger, she didn't feel like she'd grabbed anything at all. She slid the finger into her mouth and giggled like a little girl at the sweetness that filled it.

"Like it?"

"It's like eating a cloud." She took another finger of the stuff. "Is this the whipped cream?"

He nodded. He was grinning just as foolishly as she was, enjoying her enjoyment.

She slid her finger along the trail of spilled beverage and tasted that, too. Recognition was immediate: that was the rich brown drink she and Eli had when they first got into their apartment.

Hot chocolate. She'd have to tell him that she'd found out what it was called.

But that would mean she'd have to tell him about going out with Felix, and that was a conversation she wasn't eager to have.

She wasn't sure what about this time made it so different from the last two times she'd run into Felix, but it was. She shoved those thoughts aside for now and focused on trying the eggs instead. It was delicious, salty and crisp around the edges, with a middle that oozed. When Felix offered her his untouched sausage muffin and cafei, insisting that he wasn't hungry and had ordered it for her anyway, she couldn't refuse it.

"Frost loves its food," she observed when she'd recovered the urge to speak.

"It helps to have enough," he agreed.

The doll flounced back to the edge of their table. "How is everything?"

Felix grinned at it, looking just as happy as Ember had yet seen him. "Everything's great."

Ember waited for the doll to move away again before speaking. She sensed the time had come to broach the real subject, but she knew she had to be careful about it — she didn't want to toggle Felix's switch that turned him from eager to closed-off by saying anything wrong.

"The dolls," she started at last, attempting a slightly sideways entry into the topic. "There's a lot of them here?"

"Oh, lots," he answered, but then hesitated, and his voice came out just a little more slowly when he spoke again. "Why?"

Ember poked at her plate, dragged her fork through the leftover ooze from the eggs. "Well, some of them aren't working right, and the queen wants me to fix them. But I can't figure out what's wrong with them. I'm not a scientist, not like my father — I just like to tinker with things. I was wondering..." She hesitated. Maybe she was pushing a little too far, creeping a little too close to things that would shut Felix up entirely, but since she was already here, there was no reason not to at least try.

She took a breath and decided to go for it. "They say the wall is cracking. But I don't know what that means, and I can't get anyone to tell me."

Felix's face drained of color, and he stared at her for a long moment with the same kind of shock she'd seen on the queen's face when repeating the dolls' words to her. His voice, when he seemed to have finally recovered it, came out thin and surprisingly harsh. "They're talking about the wall?"

"The ones they say are malfunctioning, yes." She hesitated a moment, considered, then pressed on with a bit more decisiveness. "Is it cracking?"

Felix shook his head. "It can't be. That's not … not possible. But dolls — they don't lie."

"You know which wall they're talking about?"

He blinked at her, long and slow. "There's only one it could be."

Chapter Sixteen

THEY SLIPPED OUT of the cafe, though the doll, of course, noticed their passing — how could it not when the bell hanging at the top of the door chimed when it opened. It smiled that absurd smile of all the dolls and waved one human-looking hand. "Come back soon, dears!"

Felix gave it a quick grin. Ember just walked through the door and out into the cool streets without acknowledging it.

It was edging toward daylight now. Though the electrics were still the primary source of light on the roads, the sky had melted from the inky black of proper night toward the grayish blue of nearing sunrise. Ember wasn't sure when, exactly, she was expected to return to the workshop, or the palace, or wherever she was supposed to go for her day's work, but at this point, she didn't really care.

"The wall?" she prompted in a whisper when Felix hesitated outside the door of the cafe.

He looked back at her, his expression deadly serious. "We're not supposed to go to the wall. Getting too close might interfere with the magic."

She let the mention of magic slide. "I just want to see it. To know what the dolls are talking about, so I can fix them," she added when Felix didn't look convinced. "I couldn't tell what was broken in them yesterday, but if I could see what they were talking about…"

She let the sentence fade off before she had to come up with the way to properly end it. She didn't actually know if seeing the wall could help her understand what was wrong with the dolls, but if she didn't let on about that, maybe that was a believable reason.

Maybe it would be enough.

Or maybe Felix would tell her to go back to wherever she came from and stop bugging him with mysteries that weren't hers — or his — to solve.

She smiled, aiming for guileless, and widened her eyes just a little. She'd seen people flirt before, but she'd never done it herself. She'd never had anyone to flirt with before, and she was pleased to see Felix's face once again tinge pink under the expression. "Please? Just for a minute? I only want to look."

Felix bit his lip. She could see him wavering, uncertain. A desire to show her something, give in to her request, maybe even his own curiosity, warring behind his eyes with the apparently ingrained belief that no one should do what she was asking of him.

She slid a little closer to him, close enough that she could feel the warmth coming off his skin, that she could, if she wanted, reach out and take his hand. Her fingers twitched, but she folded them together and forced them still. "Do you know what's on the other side?"

"Nothing," he answered, too quickly.

"You sure?"

"It's the end of the world. There's nothing beyond the wall."

"But what if there was?"

His curiosity was winning — she could see that spark, that light, that came on inside of him when she'd touched on something interesting.

She dared to needle just a little more. "It can't hurt to look, can it? If there's nothing there, what is there to be afraid of?"

Felix let out a breath, big enough that it puffed visible in the air before floating away. "We can't get too close. It might interfere with the magic that holds it up."

Ember nodded.

He reached out, bolder than before, and took her hand, then turned halfway around and tugged her along after him. "This way."

Felix dropped her hand after a couple of steps without looking at her, and walked with sudden purpose away from the cafe and toward what Ember thought was in the direction of the palace square for a couple of blocks before turning right and heading east.

They went only another block before taking a left, then another left, so they were going west, then a third left like he was determined to take them in a circle.

He took the turns sharply, as if deciding on them midstride, and there was an intentionality that Ember couldn't make out to it. Finally, after another few blocks and a new easterly direction, she had to ask which direction they were actually meaning to go.

"South," Felix answered in a whisper almost too low to hear.

"South?" she repeated with a pointed glance at the sunrise brightness visible directly in front of them.

Felix peeked over his shoulder, quick and furtive. "We're being followed."

Ember looked behind her. There was a small stream of

people in the streets with them, at least half of them going in the same easterly direction as they were. No one seemed particularly suspicious — she just saw the same doll smiles and half-interested expressions that she'd seen on most of the Frost citizens so far. "How—?"

Felix grinned wryly, interrupting her question before she'd even finished asking it. His voice stayed well below a whisper, barely loud enough to make out even as Ember was listening for it. "I've spent at least half my life dodging a tail."

She dropped her own voice to match his. "Why?"

"My father works for the queen."

Was that all it took to get someone followed?

Felix glanced over his shoulder again, then turned to face straight into the sun, squinting slightly. "The short man in the brown hat, about twenty steps behind us."

Ember looked again. There were a couple of people moving in a small clump with the same sense of purpose as them. Behind those people, she could just glimpse the man Felix was talking about: a doll dressed in the Frost men's usual attire, shorter and somewhat rounder than the other people on the street. Their eyes met. Its attention was fixed on her, its smile blank and empty.

She swallowed hard. She'd seen that sort of doll before — it was the same kind as the trolley drivers she'd seen, practically identical except that this one wore a man's hat.

"Alexei," Felix muttered. "Not too bright. Shouldn't be hard to—"

He took another sharp turn east, then darted into a tiny space between two windowless brick walls. He pulled Ember into the space beside him and held one finger to his lips.

Ember froze, barely even daring to breathe, as she

pressed instinctively to Felix's side and waited to see what the doll would do.

Between the walls, in the space where she could just make out the street they'd just been on, she could see the doll, their tail, its smile undeterred as it passed blithely by their hiding spot.

Felix watched it go, peering out past the opening for a moment, then grinned at Ember. "Alexei," he whispered, his words going nearly directly into her ear. "Not the Envoys' brightest and best."

They slipped out of the space and took the road back the way they'd come at a half-run. After another block and a few small clusters of people separated them from the doll, Felix let out a breath and smiled. "Someone must've overheard," he said, though Ember wasn't sure if he'd meant the words for her or not. Then he glanced over at her, his grin turning playful. "They always get weird when people start talking about going places."

"Why would we be followed now?" Ember wondered, keeping her voice low so the people around them couldn't hear.

Felix shrugged. "We were followed the entire time the other day, out to the old city."

"What?" Ember stopped walking, startled by this news. Being followed was something she'd been watching for, even expecting, and the fact that she hadn't seen anyone doing it was part of what had her so on edge.

Felix paused only for a moment, then kept walking, his forward movement pulling Ember's legs back into working. "Yeah. The guy sitting across from us on the trolley? I don't know if he followed you to and from your place, but he was following us from the square to the old city and back."

"I ... didn't notice," Ember admitted. Her face felt

warm. So much for her powers of observation — that was a pretty big thing for her to have overlooked.

Felix shrugged again as if this was nothing to comment on. "Most of the time, an Envoy tail isn't anything to worry about. The man probably just went back to the Envoy office, wrote out a detailed report about you being fascinated by the light posts, and stuck the paper in a drawer somewhere where no one will ever see it again."

"The Envoy office," Ember repeated slowly, certain that she'd heard the words before. "Isn't that where your father works?"

Felix grinned his acknowledgment.

Ember felt something click into place inside her thoughts. It wasn't that she was necessarily bad at spotting something like the fact someone was following her — it was that Felix was particularly skilled at it, probably because it was his father's job to be or assign people to tail others. The heat in her face lessened somewhat, cooled by a flash of relief.

She hadn't thought to feel lucky about meeting this particular Frost boy, but now she suspected she might be. What were the chances that someone who knew about how the city actually worked was the one who'd approached her in the square the other day, the one who'd become her...

Friend, she decided. That's what they were, friends.

It warmed something deep inside her to allow herself to think that. She didn't go around applying that label to people who didn't deserve it — to date, Eli, and maybe old Korrah, were the only people she could use the word with.

It felt good to use it for Felix.

The drifting crowd around them was peeling away noticeably now, people turning off the southbound street into buildings or other streets, and before Ember was quite ready for it, they were the only two people left heading south. And then the buildings stopped, and they were facing a giant wall.

At first, Ember wasn't sure exactly what it was she was looking at. Unlike every other built thing inside Frost, it lacked the sort of perfection she was getting used to seeing. Lumpy and whitish and so massive that it took a moment for her brain to catch up with what her eyes were seeing and put a word to it.

It was a wall. A wall of ice — but not the clear bluish ice smooth as glass like the palace was built from. This ice was more like the sort she was used to seeing: a dirty off-white studded with lumps and seams where bricks were laid on top of each other and gaps filled in with snow. The entire thing rose straight into the air and disappeared through the shimmer of the force field. To both sides, right and left, was an apparently endless expanse of the same dirty ice wall.

"What...?" she began, but then found that she didn't have the words to finish her question. She stared down for a moment in one direction, trying to find an end to the wall, then in the other when that way disappeared over the horizon before ending.

There was, as far as she could tell from here, no place where the wall actually stopped.

She took a couple of steps forward, crossing the sudden edge of the city buildings with her hand raised as though to touch the wall, perhaps just to reassure herself that she was actually seeing a thing she thought she was seeing.

Felix pulled in a sharp breath. "Don't," he said suddenly, grabbing Ember's arm.

Ember looked back at him; his eyes kept shifting around as though he wasn't sure what he could or could not safely rest his gaze on. She turned completely toward him, letting her raised hand fall back to her side. "Felix? You okay?"

His shifting eyes wouldn't settle. He shook his head.

"What's wrong?"

"You promised not to get close."

She didn't recall making any promise of the sort, but she didn't push it — he was obviously nervous, maybe even afraid, and she sensed he'd taken some kind of strange risk already just bringing her here that she didn't want to reward his bravery, or curiosity, with regret.

She stepped back into the safety of that invisible line, and the tension in Felix's shoulders and jaw visibly relaxed. "Okay. I'm sorry. I'm not going to touch it."

"We can't interfere with the queen's magic. If the wall falls, we all do."

Ember looked back at the wall. It was a shocking sight, but Frost was full of shocking sights. And this one, though too big for her mind to comprehend, was almost shockingly normal aside from that fact. Blocks of ice — and not even flawless blue Frost ice. Just regular, everyday, dirty white ice plastered together with melted and refrozen snow, built just the way that every wall and home in Dusk was built.

She couldn't see any cracks, besides the ones mortared up with snow and ice, but she couldn't see it all, either, not the top nor the ends.

And she knew that her not being able to see cracks didn't mean there weren't any there.

"Why?" she asked at last, her voice falling to a whisper. "What's behind it?"

"Nothing." The answer came too fast, like a rehearsed and regurgitated answer. But then Felix repeated it, perhaps in response to the frown Ember could feel forming on her face. "Nothing. The world ends here."

Felix's gaze finally settled, and it settled on Ember. He stared into her eyes with a fierceness she couldn't quite interpret, something that was clearly meant to mean more than he was saying, but she didn't know what. "If the wall falls, we all do," he repeated.

And then his voice fell, his whisper turning to barely more than a breath. "Here, there be dragons."

Chapter Seventeen

THERE WERE HALF a dozen dolls waiting for Ember in the workshop that day. Three of them were sitting quietly in chairs and smiling blankly at nothing; the other three were standing or pacing and muttering to themselves despite Vallenovich's order to sit down and be quiet. One of them was clawing at the walls of the workshop with its fingers as if trying to dig its way out of the room.

Ember balked. The dolls yesterday had been a disturbing sight, but they'd sat still and said very little.

Whatever was happening to them, it looked like it was getting worse.

Vallenovich waved Ember toward her charges. "Go on, *devushka.*"

Somehow, strangely, his tone reminded her of Felix's earlier that morning, whispering to himself.

Here, there be dragons.

Ember grabbed a pair of pliers so that her fingers had something to hold on to, and she marched toward the dolls with all the boldness she could summon.

They were mechanical people. Surely, they couldn't hurt her.

She started with the moderate dolls, the ones who were sitting and smiling. It only occurred to her after the first doll crumpled to the floor that perhaps it was a bad idea.

The wild doll, the one clawing at the walls, actually paused and turned to her when the first mild-mannered one dropped. Its eyes widened, and now, looking them in the face, she realized something she hadn't noticed before.

It was Maudie.

But that didn't make any sense. Maudie had brought her to Vallenovich just a few minutes ago.

Had the doll madness taken her so fast? Or — and Ember shuddered to think it — were there many Maudies in the city? Dolls who all looked exactly alike, and the only way to tell one from the other was by which ones had gone mad?

"What are you doing?" the Maudie doll asked, eyes skipping from the deactivated doll at Ember's feet to Ember herself. Its face seemed pale. Afraid.

Ember stepped toward it, being careful not to bump the doll at her feet as she did so. She held out a hand. She couldn't say why, but the gesture felt right, an extension of peace, an attempt to understand and help. "Maudie?"

The doll frowned. The expression looked very odd on a face that she was used to seeing covered by a dazzlingly bright smile. For all that its actions, the desperate, barely audible mumbling, made the doll seem mad, its voice was now level. Sane. "Ember Mikailanova."

She glanced over at Vallenovich. He'd taken a seat on the other side of the room and was watching her, but with a disinterested glaze over his expression, like he wasn't actually paying much attention. She took another step toward the Maudie and let her voice drop to a whisper, too quiet for her handler to overhear. "How do you know my name?"

The doll blinked. Once. Twice. "He told me. He said you'd come."

"Who did?"

"The prince of Sand. He's waiting for you."

"You're not here to talk to them!"

Vallenovich was at her side, his voice booming in the quiet space. He grabbed Ember's arm, fingers tight and shaking, and yanked her back from the doll, turning her halfway around to face him, and pointed at the doll. "Turn them off."

"Let go of me," Ember snapped back.

"Turn them off!"

She wrenched her arm out of his grip. All the dolls were watching them, faces blank, even the ones who were standing up and muttering to themselves.

Vallenovich snatched the pliers out of her hand, spun hard toward one of the sitting dolls, and jammed the plier tips gracelessly into the back of its head. The doll's face went completely slack for a moment, even its blank smile dropping away from its lips, and then it slumped over into the lap of the doll sitting beside it.

"I don't know why we even have you here," Vallenovich said. His voice was rough. "It's easy enough to turn these things off."

He jammed the pliers into the next doll's head.

The Maudie doll shrieked.

"No! What're you—" A stupid question; Ember cut herself off before finishing it. "You're hurting them!"

"You should be fixing them."

"There's nothing *wrong* with them!"

The third quiet doll collapsed under Vallenovich's frustrated jabs. Through the curtain of hair at the backs of their heads, Ember could see something sparking, some of their electrics damaged.

Vallenovich spun around, reaching now for the pacing couple of dolls, who had stilled at his actions and watched him with fear blazing out of their human-like eyes.

"Wait! Wait. Is there some place where we can look at their … their coding or something? Maybe we can figure out who's sending the signals that are making them malfunction?"

It was a desperate idea, not so much a plan as a stray thought — Ember didn't even know if the dolls ran on signals or programming or what, and she certainly wasn't equipped to figure things out looking at software — but it stopped Vallenovich's rampage in its tracks, and when he looked at her again, there was something other than annoyance in his face.

Hope sparked in Ember's head. Maybe there was something to that — maybe there was some kind of signal targeting the dolls. Maybe they were malfunctioning not because of some hardware problem, but because something was messing with their programming.

"Where are the logs kept?" she asked, like she knew there had to be logs. It was a trick she'd learned some time ago about making herself seem like she knew better what was going on than she actually did: to speak an assumption or suspicion like an obvious fact.

And it worked. Vallenovich didn't dispute the idea of logs, and he lowered the pliers. The Maudie doll quieted at the end of his rampage, went from shrieking to staring — which wasn't exactly less uncomfortable, but at least wasn't adding to the panic racing through Ember's limbs.

Ember took a breath, tried to gentle the frantic pace of her heart. "Maybe it isn't something wrong with their heads," she offered, mostly to keep Vallenovich's attention on her. "Maybe there's a signal that's the problem. Where do the dolls' orders come from?"

Vallenovich blinked. "What do you want with their orders?"

"I want to see them. Maybe there's something there."

He came toward her, pliers half-raised like he was thinking of jamming them into the back of her head. His eyes flashed, and his voice had fallen to a rough whisper. "You're not authorized."

Ember didn't groan, but only because she caught the noise on her teeth and forced it back down. "Well, who is?"

"No one."

"So how do you keep track of the dolls' orders? Their programming?"

Vallenovich brandished the pliers, waved them like a threat in front of her face. "It's not necessary to track their orders. They do as they're told."

But Vallenovich's reaction had already told Ember what she wanted, that there were logs. Someone in Frost tracked the dolls' programming.

For the first time, Ember had something to try — something that wasn't just crumpling the dolls to the floor.

Vallenovich lowered the pliers. "Back to work, *devushka*."

Ember held her hand out for the pliers, and he gave them back to her, then turned and went back to his usual place watching her from the middle distance.

Fingers touched her arm. Ember looked up at the Maudie doll standing beside her. The doll's eyes were blank, staring, not seeing what was in front of it but focused on something Ember couldn't make out. "The prince of Sand," it whispered, too low for Vallenovich to hear. "He's calling for us."

"What—"

"The wall is cracking," the doll interrupted, unhelpfully. "It's time to go."

Chapter Eighteen

THERE WERE MONSTERS EVERYWHERE.

Ember was pretty sure this was a dream, because she was pretty sure monsters weren't real. But it was hard to tell, because the monsters looked very real indeed.

They were made of swirling, insubstantial shadows, and they refused to settle into any coherent shape — their edges shifted and blurred, morphed in and out of view, bumped against and separated from the others. They didn't seem to notice Ember there in the center of their circle, but even though they weren't trying to close in on her, they remained, an impenetrable wall of shifting shadows in every direction.

She opened her mouth, hoping she could talk to them, wondering if it was possible to reason with monsters in what she was still pretty sure was a dream. But no words came out.

She felt the shadows' curiosity suddenly directed at her, as if the simple movement of opening her mouth had attracted their attention. *What are you?*

The same question she hope to ask of them. She could feel it directed at her now.

What are you?

Here, there be dragons.

What is a dragon?

A monster. Not real.

The last words were her father, answering her child-hood question as the two of them looked at those words written in the space between two jagged lines. She was small, barely able to talk, and he was holding her in his lap, a book cradled between his hands.

"What's a dragon?" she asked.

The room was warm, lit by a fire that gave an occasional pop as if wanting to join the conversation. Ember didn't know how it was burning — rations of firewood had run out long before she was born.

But maybe it didn't matter, because this was a dream. She sank into it happily, grateful for a moment with her father again, even if just a moment reconstructed from a long-forgotten memory.

"It's a monster," her father answered. "Not real."

"So why is it written on the map?"

"Because that's where they live."

This made sense. Of course a mapmaker would label the shore where dragons lived. She felt silly for even asking the question.

(But why would a mapmaker label the home of a monster that didn't exist?)

Ember traced the jagged line across the paper with one pudgy little-girl finger. "Where is this?"

(Beyond the edge of the world.)

Her father touched the paper. There was something written there, too, beyond the line of the dragons. Ember tried to see it, but she was a small girl. She couldn't read.

(Beyond the wall. Forest. The Leshii.)

The words made no sense.

The wall of home faded away, the warmth of the fire blinking out of existence. It was replaced by some kind of machine, a giant thing partially covered in rusting metal plates. Where the plates weren't covering up the interior of the machine, Ember could see giant cogs and gears and pistons, all of them coated with a thin layer of rust like it had been many years since the machine had worked.

But past the rust and age, Ember could only begin to see the perfect beauty and intricacy of the machine.

She touched it gently on a bit of plating that was relatively smooth and not dangerously rusty. Her eyes moved up and down the lengths of the pistons, noting the notches where the cogs and gears interwove. The fits were perfect, better than any old watch or engine she'd ever seen — the coating of rust couldn't hide the elegant construction of the thing.

Her chest felt empty and tight, and tears stung her eyes. A machine this beautiful should've never gone still for so long.

As if responding to her touch, or maybe her sadness, something inside the machine began to shift, grinding like a gear struggling to shake off too many years of immobility. The plate beneath her fingers began to shiver.

You must wake the Leshii.

Ember's eyes snapped open, and for a moment, she was blinded by the lingering fragments of the dream, the slight vibrations of the metal plating beneath her fingertips. The image, the feeling, clung to her thoughts like snow in her hair.

And even as those fragments melted like snowflakes, a smear of sadness and the final words remained.

You must wake the Leshii.

She didn't know what it meant. She didn't know what the Leshii was or why it needed waking. She was just dreaming, after all, and dreams meant nothing. She was as likely to wake the Leshii as she was to return to her childhood and sit on her father's lap as he showed her the book of maps.

As likely as she was to find her father, who had died out in the tundra.

It took a few long, sleepy blinks for Ember to become fully cognizant of the space around her.

At first, she thought the trembling in the bed was her own body, reacting to whatever leftover stress remained in her muscles. But then she felt the tremor even in her temple and toes, places that didn't tremble no matter the reason, heard the rattle of glass from across the room, the faint but rising sound of people screaming from the streets, and understood.

It wasn't her that was shaking — it was the ground itself.

Ember didn't move, frozen between the urge to get up and see what was happening and the desire to bury herself into a ball beneath her fluffy white blanket and hide from the idea that the ground itself could tremble. She peered over at nothing, and wondered if the nothing could stare back.

The tremor died after a minute, and slowly, Ember peeled herself off the couch and looked out the window. A small crowd of people hurried down the street, their expressions tense and uncertain. Probably aiming toward the palace, if Ember had to take a guess at their destination.

Which seemed as useful an idea as any, so she left her room and slid into the crowd, allowing herself to be pulled along by the force of bodies moving in the same direction.

The screams had died with the trembling, but there was still a tension in the air, a silence full of fear, broken only by the occasional sob or whisper.

They did indeed end up in the square, pressing into an increasingly large crowd of people who were looking, wide-eyed and pale, at either the palace or the statue of Atalanta. A flash of orange to her left caught Ember's eye.

"Ember!" Felix called over the hum of the crowd. He shoved past the last few people — dolls, still somehow smiling — between them. "Are you okay?"

"I'm okay." Ember scanned Felix from head to foot. From what she could tell, he seemed unhurt. "You?"

"I'm fine. A little rattled."

"The wall is cracking!"

The voice, nearly a scream, lifted above the panicked hum of the crowd.

Ember turned toward the sound, and so did a number of others. It was a doll speaking — that didn't surprise her — a female-presenting one who was scrambling now to climb the Atalanta statue in the center of the square.

"The wall is cracking!" it yelled again. "It won't be long now."

Several hands reached for the doll and tore it off the statue. They all disappeared into the crowd, though Ember could still make out the sounds of the doll trying to repeat its message, though now its words were strangely mumbled and incoherent, the sounds that made up those words switching places with each other so nothing made sense from its mouth.

Beside her, Felix frowned. Fear crept into the expression.

The doll he had pushed aside turned its smile on them. "There's no need to fear. The queen protects us."

Felix blinked, and a little of the tension in his face relaxed. "I know. I trust the queen."

"As you should," the doll agreed. Its voice was low, even, soothing.

But Ember was not so easily pacified by the assurances of a doll. She frowned at it. If she opened up its head, would she see something different from the dolls that had gone mad, the ones she'd deactivated inside the palace?

She doubted it. She'd never seen inside a working doll's head, but from how well-made the malfunctioning ones looked, she still wasn't yet convinced the issue was their parts.

The doll smiled back at her. "It's all right. There's nothing to fear."

Nothing but the ground becoming unstable under people's feet and the dolls screaming for some reason about cracks in the wall, she thought, though she didn't speak the words aloud.

The crowd shifted, stilled. The palace doors opened, and the queen, accompanied by an impressive entourage of guards and white-suited men crossed the bridge toward the square.

The crowd parted for them when they reached the other side of the bridge, obeying the silent gestures from a couple of dolls. The one who'd been talking to Ember spread its arms and stepped back, forcing Ember and Felix to do the same as the queen and her guards passed them.

The queen walked silent and graceful through the parted crowd, her head up, her eyes forward, never looking around, probably not even making eye contact with anyone around her. She reached the Atalanta statue, held out one hand toward a guard, and took the spear the man offered her. Then, just as slowly and gracefully as she'd walked, she got up on the pedestal and finally turned to face the crowd.

The whole square had fallen eerily silent the moment the queen had stepped out of the palace — now, faces lifted, and the silence turned from awed to anticipatory. The queen lifted the spear, and her position mimicked Atalanta behind her so perfectly it could only have been an intentional gesture.

Ember bit the inside of her lip, all too aware of the doll just in front of them and the worshipful crowd pressed at their sides and backs. Even Felix, who Ember thought had more sense than many of the other Frost citizens, was staring at the queen like one might expect a priestess to stare at the face of Mother Atalanta herself.

Ember wasn't religious, but even Dusk had its priestesses, and she'd seen that look on their faces before. It disturbed her to see it here, for the queen of Frost who was so forcefully usurping Atalanta's rightful place.

"My people," the queen began at last, and one woman just behind Ember began to sob. "There is nothing to fear here. Have I not always protected you, cared for you, loved you?"

She paused, and a flurry of noise answered her. Words were dulled by the sound, but it was still unequivocal agreement. Felix beamed, his smile as wide as any doll's, and his eyes just as strangely blank.

Ember found herself focusing on her friend more than the queen. She'd often thought of him as having a switch inside him that sometimes flipped, turning him from the warm and curious boy she liked to a dutiful citizen that didn't ask questions or wonder about any of the oddities around him. The queen's appearance had done something similar, only instead of a flipping switch, it was like he was possessed by the mindless programming of a doll.

"I will never fail you, my people. You have put your

trust, your faith, in me, and I am grateful and humbled by that. We are safe."

The woman behind Ember sobbed a little louder. A few other people cheered. Felix stared.

Ember touched his arm. "Hey," she whispered, pitching her voice below the hum of the crowd to avoid notice. "You alright?"

He didn't answer her, didn't even seem to notice she was there.

"Felix?"

"As long as the wall stands, nothing can harm us," said the queen above the crowd, the spear once again hoisted in the air like Atalanta over the boar. "We are strong. We are brave. *We are Frost!*"

A cheer, thick with emotion, ripped through the crowd as the queen came down from the statue pedestal.

The crowd parted again for her. The nearest doll spread its arms and pushed them back as the queen and her entourage started back to the palace. Felix, as if on instinct, lifted a hand towards her, and she brushed his fingers with her own as she passed.

"All's well," the doll murmured to no one in particular. "The queen will protect us."

Vallenovich, a part of the queen's tail, paused in front of them. He grasped Felix's still-outstretched hand with a smile warmer than anything Ember had seen on him before. "All right there, son?"

Felix nodded, his eyes still far away and not apparently seeing anything.

Ember wasn't sure if she should be surprised to hear the fatherly concern in Vallenovich's question. She hadn't exactly thought that Vallenovich could've been Felix's father, but it didn't strike her as odd or surprising that he was. Felix had mentioned his father was an Envoy, the head of the doll department, and seeing them next to each other, their similar shades of red hair and facial features made their relatedness impossible to miss.

Vallenovich patted Felix's hand, then turned slightly to catch Ember's eye. "Come with me, *devushka*," he said. "We've got work to do."

Chapter Nineteen

THE STREAM of dolls didn't stop that day.

Ember had almost gotten used to the idea of deactivating dolls. Even half a dozen dolls like had been there just the day before. But when she and Vallenovich stepped into the workshop and found it almost as crowded as the square outside had been, all with dolls that were screaming over top each other that the wall was cracking until the walls were quite literally shaking with their voices, well — even Vallenovich looked disturbed by this turn.

He tried to stifle it, though. Tried to clear his throat and straighten out his expression so it looked like he wasn't at all worried about anything. "Get to work," he ordered, as if it was at all that simple.

There wasn't much else Ember could do, so she went over to the dolls and started turning them off, one by one.

And the moment one of them was taken out of the room, another was brought in to replace it.

There'd never been a moment when Ember liked what she was being asked to do. Never a day when she wasn't forced to wonder if she was being a serial murderer by turning off the dolls. But she'd never felt so much like a monster as she did today, as doll after helpless doll dropped to the floor at her feet and more came in as fast as others dropped.

She lost count of them somewhere in the twenties. She lost all ability to feel somewhere in the forties. The only thing that kept her moving at all was the promise of an idea burrowing its way out of her brain. A spark of hope, the first corners of a thought.

Perhaps it was all connected: the mysterious doll madness, the dreams, the cracking wall. All of it, coming from a single source.

The Maudie doll she'd spoken to yesterday had mentioned someone. The prince of Sand. He was, apparently, waiting for her.

The timing of it all, the strange coincidence of all these things happening at once — it didn't escape her notice.

If she could just get over the wall, find out what was behind it that the queen was so determined to keep hidden that she had everyone in her city convinced that the world ended there, maybe some of this would start to make sense.

But she'd seen the wall. It was huge. Impenetrable. There was no way she'd be able to climb it, or burrow through it, or under it. And it wasn't as if she could fly over it.

Unless…

Unless she could get her hands on a copter.

The thought nearly stilled her hands, nearly interrupted the grim flow of her work, stunning her into immobility.

She knew where she could find copters. Lots of them. And yes, they'd looked broken from the view she had of them through the window of the cathedral, but there were so many of them — perhaps one or two weren't unfixable. Maybe there were parts enough to scavenge up an entire working copter.

And if she could get one of those copters working, she could fly over the wall and finally see what was on the other side.

EMBER EXPECTED the door to be locked. It was clear to anyone who wanted to look that these copters were being set apart from the public, and it seemed to her that if they had the capacity — solid doors, working latches — it was foolish to not lock those doors.

But the door pushed open under her hand with only a little bit of applied force. The wood nearly splintered at the edges of her hand and didn't move again once she'd wedged it open far enough for her and Felix to slip through.

They were in the main room with the copters. There was a lot more space inside, between the almost-touching passenger bubbles, than she'd thought looking into it from the window, and she ducked between two copters toward their fronts.

Felix followed. His eyes were strained wide, his face pale, but still a grin tugged relentlessly on one corner of his mouth. "We really shouldn't," he whispered.

Ember grinned back. "You keep saying that."

"It keeps being true."

"And yet, here we are."

"Here we are," he echoed. He looked around, gaze snagging on the copters first as the primary thing in the room, but then drifting up toward the domed ceiling, where his own grin finally broke free of its restraints. "Oh. It's just as beautiful on the inside."

Ember glanced toward the ceiling. It was high and painted with fading chips of color. Impressive, certainly, but she was much more interested in the broken copters than the ceiling.

Felix took a few steps away, farther into the room, staring at the ceiling the whole time, and Ember didn't try to pull his attention back.

Both of them wanted to be here. The fact that they had different reasons for it wasn't important.

She focused on the copters. From the outside, they'd looked identically broken, stripped equally of their blades, but on closer inspection, she found one of them that hadn't had the rotating mechanism mangled in the process, and the stumps of blades still clung to the mechanisms.

Ember poked around the room, checking occasionally to make sure that Felix hadn't wandered off entirely and left her — no, he was as engaged with the ceiling dome and faded old artwork as she was with the copters. In one dark corner, stacked in the space between a copter and the wall, she hit a real boon.

Blades.

Whoever had taken the blades off the copters had tossed those blades into one corner like they thought that would end their usefulness forever.

Ember yanked and pulled and with great effort was able to get the stack a little away from the wall and toward the light coming in through windows and oculi. Most of the blades looked as broken as the stumps left over on one of the copters, but a few seemed whole.

"What're you doing?" Felix asked. He came over from the far southern wall where he'd been staring reverently at some portrait or something, upon hearing the sound of metal blades scraping over stone.

"Some of these aren't broken." Ember held out one

blade, a quarter of the total for the tail, but that had an untouched latch for securing it into the rotating bits.

Felix looked over the pile with one eyebrow raised. "You think you can find a whole set?"

"Why not?"

"It's junk."

She smiled. "And this building is an abandoned pile of bricks."

He straightened as if to start in on her about how terrible that opinion was, but then blinked as understanding spread across his face. "Ah. Point taken." Still, his skeptical eyebrow remained. "What are you going to do with all this totally-not-junk?"

"There's really only one thing to do, isn't there? I'm going to fix up a copter."

Felix shifted back like her words were a physical blow. "What? Why?"

Ember returned to rummaging through the bits of broken blades, looking for another one with an intact latching piece. Maybe there was a way for her to combine the broken pieces for some length if she needed it, but the bit that fit into the rotation piece needed to be manufactured if she could ever hope to trust flight in one of those things.

Then, realizing that Felix was still waiting for an answer, she gave him one. "I'm going over the wall, of course."

Chapter Twenty

DAYS PASSED. Night was coming increasingly quick and lingering increasingly long, so that even if the sun did come out, Ember wasn't able to see it from her place in the doll workshop.

A few times, the queen came for her and demanded that she fix her wall machines, but with each visit, Ember became increasingly sure that whatever was causing the ice to crack, it wasn't the fault of the machines.

On the third visit, she made another attempt to tell the queen just that. "I can't find anything wrong with them."

The queen frowned and paused at the door between the dark little hallway and the rest of the palace, her fingers just grazing the knob. She didn't answer.

"The machines," Ember prompted. "There doesn't appear to be anything wrong with them."

The queen's frown deepened. She turned the knob and stepped into the palace, still without answering.

Ember followed, unsure of what else she could do. A part of her felt sorry for the queen — it must seem to her like everything she'd spent her life building was crumbling around her ears.

The other, larger part of her was frustrated with being told to fix things that weren't broken.

"I didn't want to say until I was sure," she hedged.

Again, the queen didn't answer — she just kept walking, her pace as brisk as it ever was, her eyes forward and unmoving, forcing Ember to either keep up or fall behind and making it perfectly clear that the queen herself didn't care which one Ember chose.

Ember elected to fall behind, and when the queen turned a corner, she didn't follow.

After her hours in the workshop, Ember took a trolley to the old city to work on the copters. She'd found the one she wanted, where both top and tail mechanics were relatively intact, and she'd managed to scrounge up enough blades with the proper hooks and anchors to reattach them. But a few of those blades were cracked or broken, and it took her a couple of days to smuggle out the right tools from the doll workshop so she had everything she needed to repair the broken spots.

She wasn't entirely sure that she needed the blades to be a particular length, but it seemed like a good idea to match them as best she could. She drilled and screwed and hammered at the blades long into the night, often stopping only when Felix, who always came with her, warned her that if they didn't go now, they'd miss the last trolley back.

Ember wasn't entirely sure why Felix came with her to the cathedral. Of course she understood that he had his own fascination with the building itself, and a lot of times, she would look up from her work to stretch out a kink in her neck and find him gone, wandering into other rooms, and when he came back, he would be shivering with delight about what he'd seen. But he must've looked at everything there was to see after a couple of visits, yet he still elected to come with her, and increasingly he would sit beside her, holding her tools or helping her with an unwieldy piece of blade, while she worked.

"What do you think is on the other side?" he asked one night when they both sat back after a tricky bit of repair.

Ember wiped the sweat from her brow and looked over at him. Felix so rarely mentioned even the possibility of *something* existing beyond the wall, usually trying to insist on the Frost party line that there was *nothing*, that the question felt significant, and she wanted to answer it right. Honest, doubtful, but without toggling his curiosity switch.

"I don't know. Something the queen doesn't want people to see."

Felix swallowed and looked away from her, his curiosity warring with his brainwashing.

Ember bit the inside of her lip and waited. Hoping, dreading.

Finally, slowly, his eyes came back to her, though his head stayed bowed and his voice had gone small. "What do you think that is?"

Ember smiled. "That's what I wanna find out. That's why we're building the copter, yeah?"

"Yeah."

"The one thing I do know is that it's not the end of the world. Whatever's over there, it can't be the end. The world was much, much bigger than this Before. It can't be less big now."

They went back to work, silent for a while, before Felix finally said, "Tell me about Before."

So Ember told him the stories she knew about Before. About the forest and grass that used to cover the land from Frost to Dusk and beyond. About animals that scampered and flew and grazed. The libraries and cathedrals that

Ember had only ever seen in sketches and dreams — she guessed that Felix would be especially interested in those.

"I've never seen a book," Felix admitted when Ember tried to describe a library.

"Never?"

He shook his head.

This was a shock — even Ember had seen books. Her father had a small collection, relics from Before. Bound parchment pages of maps and words that neither Ember nor her father understood but that were beautiful to look at nonetheless.

So she went on a tangent to tell Felix about books. Before, they'd been common, so common that even the workers of the cities had whole shelves full of them, and libraries as big as this cathedral would be stuffed with them.

"You could find out anything from them. Whatever you wanted to know. Language, philosophy, science, even made-up stories from faraway or imaginary places."

Felix smiled sadly. "What happened? Do you know?"

"The Engine died."

"What does that mean?"

Ember shook her head. "I've never really been sure. Sometimes, like once or twice, I heard old Korrah mention the Engine. She called it something — the Leshii, I think? Apparently it was some kind of machine that made the world work, and it died."

"Broke?"

"I think so. That's what it has to mean, right? But Korrah never said it like 'broke.' She always said 'died.'"

Ember saw Eli less and less — half the time because she went straight from the workshop to the cathedral and half the time because he was already asleep when she went back to their apartment. She tried to talk to him sometimes, whisper things into the lengthening night, but he would only turn over and ignore her.

It frightened her, the thought that she might've damaged her relationship with Eli so badly that he wasn't even willing to talk to her. Worse was the fact that she wasn't even really sure what she'd done. Yes, she'd refused to go back to Dusk when he mentioned that they ought to, but was that really going to be the thing to end their life-long friendship? She'd refused to marry him this summer, and even that hadn't kept him from talking to her after-ward. They'd had awkward conversations heavy with significance that Ember didn't want to spend time examin-ing, but they'd at least happened. Eli didn't stop talking to her then, so why should he now?

She couldn't even ask him to explain, because she couldn't find him, and even when they did happen to cross paths in the halls, he didn't look at her and kept walking wherever he was going.

Well. She would let him sulk for a few days. Maybe he needed that. But surely that didn't mean he wouldn't talk to her again.

Mostly she tried to put that out of her mind, and mostly she was successful. There were still plenty of other things to do, after all.

She was growing especially worried about the dolls. The number of them coming into the workshop had gone from a half dozen a day to a half dozen an hour. Ember wasn't sure where all the deactivated ones were taken — Vallenovich just had another Envoy take them away in wheeled carts — but surely people had begun to notice by now that the dolls were acting up. Someone must've seen or heard something.

But if someone had, Vallenovich wasn't talking about it.

It took nearly three weeks and dozens of cobbled-together or stripped-and-replaced parts, but Ember thought that the copter might be about ready to try running. She knew there wasn't going to be much opportunity to practice flying the thing — she expected that, as soon as it was up in the air, she would have a couple of minutes at most to clear the wall before someone started chasing her. The noise and sight of an unauthorized copter wasn't something that could be easily ignored, no matter how eager to ignore things Frost citizens could be.

She spent one night, maybe two or three, before she'd decided that she was going to do it, playing with the levers and switches inside the passenger bubble. She'd twist one of the levers — the one she thought connected to the tail blades and controlled direction — and watch the way the tail blades tilted just barely to one side or the other. The upper blades for lift weren't so visible, so she had Felix stand outside of the bubble and tell her what was happening when she wiggled this lever or that.

"You're really going to fly it," he whispered as they closed up the cathedral behind them for the night.

"Yes. We're going over the wall, Felix. We're going to find out what the queen is hiding."

He frowned. "What do you mean? She's never hidden anything."

Ember bit back a sigh. The safety of the cathedral, out of the way and abandoned, had cracked his curiosity wide open, until he was very nearly questioning the queen herself inside there, but as soon as they stepped outside again, he toggled back into a proper Frost boy.

She tried to think of it as a good thing. Tried to use that as a reminder for her to mind her tongue when outside of the cathedral. Tried not to find it annoying, because it wasn't who Felix really was. Not what he wanted to be, and he was probably doing it to keep both of them safe from anyone who might be listening in.

"Of course," she agreed at last. "Here, there be dragons."

Felix nodded, and then didn't speak again until they were on the trolley back toward the palace.

When Ember woke the next morning, it was to several sharp, fast knocks on her door. She'd been up at the cathedral until the morning trolleys started running, reviewing and testing her repairs to her copter, trying to reassure herself that she understood everything well enough that she'd be able to fly it — maybe not well, but well enough to get her over the wall.

Felix had stayed up with her the whole night, helping where he could and talking to her where he couldn't. He hadn't even protested about missing the trolley; he'd caught the mood she was in and reflected his own anxious excitement back at her.

"We're going over the wall," he'd said when Ember finally declared the copter as finished as she could manage it.

Ember smiled. She liked that Felix had started using "we" without even thinking about it. That he seemed just as interested in the answer to what lay beyond the wall as she was. "Tomorrow," she promised.

She'd barely made it back to her room before dropping into a dreamless, exhausted sleep.

And now a hand on her shoulder was shaking her even out of that.

She wrenched open one eye, already fully aware that the person on the other side was about to get an earful of her worst self and not able to summon the energy to care. The sun hadn't even risen yet, and while it didn't rise until late morning these days, a part of her was already determining how to best point that out.

"What?" she snapped even as she was shaking herself awake enough to speak at all.

Eli stood above her, flanked by two smiling dolls. "Where have you been?"

Ember planted herself against her pillows, letting the softness of them hide half her face, and glared with the exposed eye, first at the dolls, then at Eli. "Where have *I* been? Where have *you* been?"

Eli made a sound in his throat, something halfway between a sigh and a groan, and glanced to the dolls. "Give us a minute."

"We are supposed to remain here," one of the dolls answered. His smile was nearly wide enough to touch each ear, but somehow it widened a little further, until it was a grotesque parody of even a doll's smile.

"Then do that." Eli glanced at Ember. "Come into the other room with me?"

She grumbled wordlessly into her pillow but sat up, and when Eli moved to lead her from the bedroom, she shambled along after him. The dolls, thankfully, didn't make any move to follow, and as she shut the bedroom door behind her, she glanced first from one doll to the other. Their smiles, already that strange and terrible doll smiles, stretched until their skin pulled almost to tearing. How long would it be before she saw these dolls again, deactivated under her hands in the workshop for ranting about the wall?

If the rate at which dolls were coming in kept up, it surely wouldn't be too long.

She shut the door and turned back to Eli. He looked out of place, uncomfortable. His clothes were Frost style, but ill-fitting, baggy over his hips and too tight across his shoulders, and he held his wide-brimmed hat crumpled between both hands.

Ember pressed back against the door, half to keep the dolls from opening it again and half because she needed the feeling of something sturdy at her back. She crossed her arms to hide the way her fingers wanted to shake. "What?"

"I just want to know where you've been."

"I haven't been the one avoiding you."

"Ember—"

"Don't take a tone." She struggled not to do it herself, to keep her own voice low and firm. "I've been trying to talk to you for days. You don't get to treat me like I'm the one at fault."

"I never said anything about fault."

"You were thinking it."

He couldn't deny that — it was too obviously true, and everything he was doing, the very fact that he was standing here in Frost clothes and flanked by dolls, made that clear.

"Who put you up to this?" she asked after the silence got too strained to bear. "The queen? Vallenovich?"

"I wasn't put up to it."

"Don't lie to me."

"You need to stop."

"Stop what?"

He gave her a look, something she couldn't parse. Something that didn't seem right on Eli's face because she didn't recognize what it meant.

If someone had asked her just two months ago if there was anything about Eli she didn't know, she would say no and feel thoroughly confident about the truth of that answer.

Now, she wasn't so sure. She didn't know what that look he gave her was supposed to mean.

"What you're doing," he answered. "It's dangerous."

"How do you know what I'm doing? You haven't talked to me in days."

"It's not hard to figure out, Ember." He took a step forward, released his hat with one hand to hold it out as if to touch her.

Ember couldn't step back, not with the way she was already pressed against the door, but she flinched away from his hand, and he dropped it. "That's a tone."

"I'm not trying to ... c'mon, Ember, you know that's not what I'm trying to do."

She relented, just a little. This was Eli, after all, and whatever had been done to him to make him practically a stranger to her, maybe it could be undone.

She thought of the copter, repaired and ready. She was going to fly over the southern wall tonight, perhaps even leave Frost entirely. Could she really do that without Eli? Without at least trying to convince him to come with her?

No. Things might be off between them, but he was still her best friend. The person she knew best and loved most in all the world.

Whatever was going on inside his head — it didn't have to mean the end. It didn't mean that he wasn't still in there, the kind, warm, happy person she'd grown up with.

She unfolded her arms and pushed herself a little away from the door — not taking a step, but tilting forward so Eli could see she wasn't trying to express any aversion to him. "We're going over the wall."

"What?"

"That wall to the south. I rebuilt a copter, and we're going to see what's on the other side."

Eli lifted his eyebrows. "'We?'" he repeated.

"Me and Felix."

"You've been out with Felix again?"

"Well, yeah." Why was that the detail he seemed concerned about? "Is there something wrong with that?"

"It's never struck you as strange that you think everyone is out to get you *except* the boy who keeps lurking around and waiting for you to show up where he already knows you'll be?"

Ember couldn't help but laugh at that. "You think Felix is out to get me?"

The scowl Eli had so clearly struggled to hold back finally escaped his control. "I think you ought to be more suspicious of the kid following you around."

She let out a breath. "You're being ridiculous."

"Am I? Or am I just being cautious? That thing you've always said I need to be more of."

"Ridiculous. Felix isn't like…" She hesitated, because she didn't know who Felix wasn't like. The queen? Vallenovich? That was true, she was sure, but those names wouldn't mean the same thing to Eli. He'd met the queen, sure, and even exchanged more words with her than Ember did, but he wasn't inclined to believe Ember's suspicions.

Obviously, or they wouldn't be having this conversation at all.

"Anyway, that's not the point," she said without finishing the rest of her previous thought.

"Well, then, what is?"

"The point" — she took a step toward Eli and poked his arm lightly with one finger for emphasis — "is that Frost is hiding something. Something much bigger than a few broken dolls. There's something beyond that wall, something that someone — and my bet is on the queen — doesn't want anyone to know about."

Eli exhaled, loud and slow, with a noise like a groan that he managed to catch in his throat before it fully formed. The scowl relaxed a little, and he tilted his head back and closed his eyes in an exaggerated indication of exhaustion. "Not this again," he said at the tail end of his sigh.

"What do you mean, 'this again'? I haven't—"

"You don't need to. I already know where this is going."

"But—"

"Not every mystery needs you to solve it."

She blinked, surprised by the venom leaking into his voice. She felt her dander rising, the anxious pulse of her blood zipping down the undersides of her arms, preparing her for a fight. She fought to keep her voice even, to keep herself from rising to his bait like he was so good at doing with her. "This one does."

"No. It doesn't. It's not your problem what the people of Frost do or don't believe about their city."

"Do you think that wall is the end of the world?"

"I don't care what anyone thinks about it."

"That's not an answer. Do you really think the world ends here, in Frost?"

"It's not important."

"Just answer the question!" Her voice was coming too loud, pitching too high; she forced it back down to a more normal level. "Please. Just yes or no."

Eli was quiet for a moment, his eyes on hers. She wasn't sure what he was seeing, but whatever it was, it made his shoulders relax, relenting. "No."

"Because there's the rest of the world beyond it. It doesn't make sense that the world would end just here, at the southern edge of Frost, and that somehow no one outside of Frost itself would know that. But them?" She gestured toward the glass wall, hoping to indicate the entire population of the city. "They don't know about

Before. They don't understand about electricity and machines that make the force field. They think it's all magic that keeps their city moving and alive." A new thought struck her, as bright and complete as the drive to see what was over that southern wall. She looked up at Eli, suddenly stunned by the thought. "And think — if Frost knew about things beyond their walls, they could be..." She swallowed. "The people here, they're generous because they can afford it, right? If they knew about Dusk, they could save them."

Eli didn't answer, and this, more than any words he might've spoken into the silence, surprised Ember. Because this was the sort of thing that should motivate him, make him understand what she was trying to say, prove to him that what she wanted to do was important.

The walls around Frost had to come down. The people needed to know they weren't sitting at the literal edge of the world. Because if they knew, if they understood, they could help Dusk. They could save their dying neighbors to the north. Eli could be the storybook hero he'd always secretly longed to be.

But Eli didn't say anything. There was a closed-off sort of expression on his face, one that Ember didn't recognize and didn't know what to do with, like he didn't even hear the words she was saying.

"Eli?" she ventured after a moment.

"I'm sorry."

"About what?"

He reached out and took her shoulders, gentle despite the hardness in his face. "We shouldn't have come here. You were right all along. We should go."

She'd thought him not answering her before was stranger than anything he could've said. She was wrong.

This was far stranger even than that. "But … our clothes. Supplies. We don't have them anymore."

"The packs are under the couch," he answered with a glance back at the furniture in question. "We can find more clothes."

"I don't understand."

He let his hands fall off her shoulders, one of them running down her arm to take her hand instead. "I know you, Ember," he said. "You won't let this go, not until we get out of here. I'm sorry it took me so long to realize that. So, let's go home. We made it across the tundra once — we can do it again."

She pulled away from him. It was an instinctual gesture and made mostly without her consent or control, but she knew the moment she did it that she shouldn't have. That that one little motion might just have cost her more than she could bear to pay.

There had been a time, and it wasn't even that long ago, when she and Eli had never fought. If they disagreed — which wasn't terribly uncommon, given how stubborn they both could be — they would've moved on to a different topic or found some compromise that suited them both. There had been a time when Ember thought there was nothing that they couldn't work through.

And then, at the beginning of the summer, some line had been crossed, some unspoken pact broken. Eli had mentioned love and marriage, and, since then, Ember had begun to see the cracks spreading across their friendship. For the first time, there was a topic they couldn't touch, a disagreement they could compromise away.

And now, with the simple motion of pulling her hand out of his, she saw the cracks between them opening into a chasm she wasn't sure either of them would be able to cross.

She looked at Eli, forcing herself to meet his eyes — because, if she was going to do this, she deserved to see the hurt it would leave in its wake. Her vision blurred through tears. "I'm sorry, Eli," she whispered, meaning it. "But I can't go with you."

Chapter Twenty-One

EMBER LEFT the room as quickly as she could without feeling too much like the ice-cold bitch she sensed that she might actually be and scurried down the spiral staircase and out into the street before her regret could catch up with her. She did her best to put Eli's hurt as far from her mind as she could.

She couldn't think about it now. If she did, that sparkling resolve, that shining sense of purpose she had, would vanish, leaving her feeling useless, with no way to bring herself back from the loss.

The consequences of her decision would have to wait until after she'd seen things through; she knew they would be there, waiting. Eager to pounce when she least expected them. They could wait.

No one stopped her as she left the building and headed down the street. Somehow, she still kept expecting that there would be, that at some point, someone would have to finally decide that she had no business out on Frost's peaceful streets and to go back to her room and wait for a summons like a good little girl. But either someone hadn't hadn't had the time or the power to put someone to the task, or nobody really cared.

She wasn't sure which option was worse.

The lights came on as she hurried down the street, flickering once or twice as the electricity passed into the bulb and then steadied. She paused for a moment to admire the seeming magic of it, then shook herself and continued on.

It was science, not magic. She knew about electricity, even if she wasn't clear on exactly how it worked. There were machines somewhere in the city that produced the electricity, just the same as there were machines making the force field that shimmered faintly blue in the waning twilight. Just because something was hard to understand didn't mean it was magic.

She hesitated then, unsure of what her next steps should be. If she spent any time fetching Felix, would that interrupt the resolve she'd finally found in knowing what she was supposed to do?

Maybe. But she'd promised him that they would fly over the wall together. He was just as invested in what he'd see on the other side as she was, and she didn't feel like she could deny him that.

Ember turned down a few more blocks and eventually onto Felix's street. His apartment was above the place with the sign that read Alabaster Trading Co.

A stray thought crossed her mind as she took the stairs up from the Alabaster Trading Co. If Frost was the edge of the world, who was Alabaster trading with? It wasn't Dusk — there was nothing to trade in Dusk.

She doubted anyone in Frost even bothered to ask such questions. It was that, that lack of curiosity, that kept the queen able to control and lie to them all.

No one stopped her as she went up to the top floor

where Felix lived, not even to ask what she was doing strolling into a building that anyone on the street must know wasn't her own place.

Maybe they assumed it was. Maybe Frost was big enough, populated enough, that no random person walking down the street would know who did and did not belong in any particular building. The idea was strangely comforting, given the fact that she was trying to be at least somewhat illicit.

The door at the top of the stairs, Felix's door, was cracked open a few finger-widths, the top hinge a bit bent so the latch didn't fit correctly into place.

Suspicion burned through Ember's core. Had someone forced the door? The suspicions turned almost immediately to worry. If the hinge was bent recently by someone forcing open the door, maybe she shouldn't go in.

But if there was someone in there, someone worrisome enough to force a closed door with enough strength to bend a hinge, maybe she needed to go in. Maybe Felix was in trouble.

Ember tapped on the door with the back of one finger. It was a compromise that felt almost cowardly — if Felix needed her help, if there was someone inside who shouldn't be there, surely announcing herself was the least smart of her options. But if the bent hinge was just a bent hinge, the slightly opened door only opened because Felix or his father hadn't shut the door more carefully, then her bursting in expecting a fight would be unspeakably rude.

The moment of silence that followed her timid knock felt like it lasted a lifetime, but then, thankfully, she heard footsteps and saw through the gap between the door and the frame a splash of fire-red hair. Felix opened the door a moment after that.

"Ember," he said like he was surprised to see her. "What are you doing here?"

"I thought…" She began, but then hesitated, unsure. What was she doing there? She'd known when she left her room, but now that she was being asked, she couldn't quite remember why it had felt so important, so right, to come. "Can I come in?"

Felix glanced over his shoulder, the same sort of quick, furtive look he gave when he was checking them for a tail. "Um … if you want to."

She looked over his shoulder as well. The apartment, at least what she could see of it, was empty. "Should I not? Maybe we can take this to the cathedral?"

"No. No, it's fine. Come in." He stepped back and opened the door wider in invitation.

She went in, but the moment of hesitation and the way he hadn't yet smiled, as though he didn't really want her here, raised her antenna again.

It was an old saying, apparently common Before, when things like antennae existed. She wasn't sure why she thought of it now, except that it felt right. People raised their antennae when they thought there was something they needed to hear, a signal that was going out across the air that might pertain to them. You raised your antenna, and you got a message.

Ember felt her own antenna going up, waiting for whatever message Felix had for her and already certain that, whatever it was, it wasn't going to be good news.

He led her into the apartment. It was much bigger than her own, a central room with many doors — not quite as many as the living quarters of the palace, but not a lot fewer, either. The central room was wide open, studded with places to sit and tables covered in messy piles of paper. White tile floors decorated with small, patterned carpets. The ever-present glass wall on the far side.

She looked out the wall toward the palace. Though she now towered over the street, being five floors up as she was, she still couldn't see all the way out. The height made her dizzy; when Felix sat on one of the dull red chairs in the room and motioned for her to take the other, faintly yellow chair beside it, she was glad to get off her newly-liquid knees and not have to look down at the roof of the building directly across the street.

"Is there something you wanted?" Felix asked after a moment. He was sitting on the very edge of his chair, his feet flat on the floor and his legs bunched up beneath him like he thought he might need to jump up at a moment's notice.

Ember felt herself echoing the position. He still hadn't smiled, not even once, and his eyes kept straying away from her and flickering toward the front door, now fully shut, and then making quick circuits around the room before he seemed to recall himself and focus again on her. "I think it's time we go," she said after the silence got so heavy as to be oppressive.

"Go?"

"Over the wall."

That brought a smile, but not one of the warm, genuine ones she expected from him. This one was tight, too big, like something a doll might offer. "How do you plan to do that?"

"The copter." She followed his next circuit around the room, wondering what he was looking for. "I thought tonight, but now I don't think we should wait."

Another long moment of painful silence. The new false smile didn't drop off Felix's face. "Is this about..." He hesitated; the smile flickered. He had to reach for it again, hard. "What you wanted to do today?"

"I—"

"Because, if it is, you should know: I can't help you. What you want to do — it's not possible."

"Felix." She leaned forward, trying to close the distance between them without looking or sounding overly suspicious to whoever he seemed to think was watching or listening to them. Because it struck her, as his eyes made another nervous circuit around the room, that was what was wrong.

Someone, somewhere, maybe even inside this very apartment, was watching or listening. Waiting for one of them to say something they shouldn't say, do something they shouldn't do.

She couldn't see them — perhaps they were behind one of the numerous doors set into the walls around them — but she suddenly felt their eyes on her. She'd have to tread carefully.

"We've been working so hard."

He shook his head. "It won't work. There's nothing to see. Just forget about it."

"I can't." She felt that tugging, deep down inside her, pulling at her, begging her to follow. "It's not just about … that. It's Eli, too."

There. She said it. The reason it had to be now, why she couldn't let herself get talked out of it under any circumstances.

Felix's eyebrows pulled down into a frown, and while Ember didn't think Felix's face was meant for frowning, at least it was better than that doll smile. "What's wrong with Eli?"

"That's just it — I don't know. But he … he's not himself."

That wasn't close to it by half, but it was the best she could manage without actually saying words that might cause trouble.

"And you think … that … will help?"

"It has to. Frost … it's not good for him."

"My father will be home soon," Felix said, changing the subject with an abruptness that actually threw her a little off balance. He stood. "You should go."

Ember stood, too, and followed him to the door. It drooped on the bent hinge, twisting the entire thing askew.

Ember glanced at the hinge. "When did that happen?"

Felix shrugged. "It was like this when I came in."

She looked at him, eyebrows raised.

He shook his head. "This hinge has been falling out of place ever since we moved in."

That was a lie, but one told very deliberately, to be heard as a lie.

"Can it be fixed?" She hoped he could hear the question she actually meant underneath the words. *Are you okay?*

He looked her straight in the eyes, and his expression did something she couldn't quite understand, but that suggested he did hear her real concern. "Probably." *Yes. Probably.*

"Should I take a look at it?" *Should I stay?*

"No!" He nearly shouted the word, then cleared his throat and tried again, more levelly. "I mean, there's no need."

Ember looked around the apartment again. It was still just as empty as it had appeared this entire time, but she again felt the invisible eyes that must be on them. She needed to get him out of this place, to somewhere safe, before something happened to him.

The possibility hadn't occurred to her until this moment, but now that it was in her head, it seemed like a very real threat. It wasn't just her own hide that could be in trouble — Felix could be, too. Maybe someone was already in the apartment, just waiting for her to leave, before they swapped him out with a mechanical double and brought him who-knew-where to do who-knew-what to him.

She reached for his hand suddenly, grateful that he didn't flinch away, and closed her fingers tight around it.

He squeezed her hand and gave her half a smile — a half-smile that looked nothing short of terribly frightened.

"Ember—" he began.

"Let's go," she interrupted in a whisper that hopefully wouldn't carry past his ear. "Please. Before something happens."

"I can't."

"It's not safe here. You know that. Please. I can't lose you."

He blinked, once, twice, as if struggling with the implications of that statement. She hadn't meant for the words to come out, but they were out now, and she didn't want to take them back.

He lifted his free hand and slowly, hesitantly, let the tips of his fingers brush against her cheek. Light as the touch was, Ember felt it down to her bones, down to the deepest part of her that tugged her toward something she didn't understand.

She didn't think that something was him, exactly, but that hardly mattered. He was a part of it. Meant to be there. Meant to be tangled up with whatever that something really was.

She leaned into the touch and closed her eyes. In the darkness, the sound of her heart thumping madly in her ears was nearly the only thing she could focus on.

That, and the faint brush of Felix's fingers against her skin.

"Please don't," he breathed, and he was so close that she could feel the words tickle against her face. "Please. It's not possible."

She opened her eyes. His gaze was fixed on her, expression equal parts worry and pleading.

And, in that expression, the spell broke.

Ember pulled away. Felix let his hands drop back to his sides. "You won't come."

"I'm sorry. Ember, please—"

"No, it's okay. I understand."

"Please don't. Please, I'm begging you, forget about it. Isn't Frost enough?"

This summer, she would've said yes. Frost was more than she could ever imagine. A place with food enough that strangers offered people apples just to be friendly, where they built amazing buildings five levels high full of warmth that came from everywhere, where the streets were clear of snow without anyone having to shovel them and people sat outside of cafes sipping hot chocolate and eating muffins and nights were lit with electricity. It was incredible, and just a couple of months ago, it absolutely would've been enough.

But there was more out there, more that the queen wasn't sharing and the people weren't asking about. Ember was restless, desperate to find out what that more was. She needed to see over the wall. Find Sand. Break whatever spell was holding her friends captive to the city.

She wanted Felix to come with her, but she couldn't force him. If he chose to stay, that was his decision to make, and it was her responsibility to accept that and not push.

"Don't go, Ember. Please."

She leaned forward and kissed his cheek. "Thank you for everything. Take care of yourself, okay?"

She was on the trolley heading toward the old city before the next round of tears caught up with her. She tried to stifle them, mindful as she was of the people riding the trolley with her, including half a dozen blank-eyed, smiling dolls. She leaned against the window of the trolley, pointed her face deliberately toward the street, and made herself swallow back the noises that wanted to escape her mouth. The faint hum of conversation rippled around her, and the wind whipping through the trolley helped to cover what sounds did manage to escape.

This was a bad idea — the whole thing, from top to bottom. If only she hadn't let Eli talk her into this mad fantasy of his, none of this would've happened.

But she knew, even as she felt regret settle heavy and painful in her gut, that she couldn't go back. Not to Dusk, maybe not ever again. She'd had a taste of what life could be like outside of the cold, dark, dying walls of that stubborn, hopeless village, and she knew that she could never go back to that again, and still find the will to live like that.

She had to go forward. Get over the wall. Find out what else was out there — for herself, for Eli and Felix, perhaps even for the whole world of people she didn't even know.

She had to get to the copter.

"Hey."

Someone in the seat across the trolley's aisle shouted above the rattle of wheels and hum of wind and conversation. His eyes were fixed on the driver, as nondescript and grinning a doll as he'd looked when Ember boarded.

"Hey, driver! This isn't the Queen's Line."

Ember blinked. She hadn't been paying any attention to their surroundings, caught up as she was in her own thoughts, but as soon as the other passenger pointed it out, the fact became disturbingly obvious. Usually on the trolley to the old city, a route she'd learned was called the Queen's Line, they'd have entered the older streets by now, the ones built with the old city, perhaps even Before, where the cobbles weren't quite so perfect and there was sometimes a misplaced brick poking out of its place. She ought to be able to see the dome of the cathedral in the distance by now, its faded colors just visible between the newer glass buildings.

Instead, they were headed too far south, and in the distance where the cathedral ought to be, there was nothing but a sheer ice wall.

"Driver!" Another voice, a woman's, joined the man across the aisle in trying to get the driver's attention. "Why have we detoured from the route?"

"The wall is cracking. It's time to go."

Ember sat forward, nearly leaped to her feet, at the familiar words.

The driver had caught the doll madness.

But she couldn't deactivate him here, behind the levers of a trolley, not without risking the lives of everyone on the vehicle, including her own.

"What was that?" the man asked. "You take us back to the Queen's Line right now, or I'll report you."

The driver's eyes, what Ember could see of them, were fixed on the wall. The trolley was accelerating now, picking up speed and heedless of the intersections it blew through.

"The wall is cracking," said the doll. "It's time to go."

Ember stood up. The trolley veered around another exchanging passengers at a stop, and a couple of people screamed as it jerked violently to the left and then right.

Ember put her arms out, bracing against the backs of the chairs as she stumbled her way forward toward the driver. "Hey," she said, lower and quieter than the other passengers had tried. "Hey, listen. You have to be careful."

The driver's eyes didn't come off the wall, which was approaching now at a terrifying speed. His smile was just as wide as it had been when she got on, but there was a manic edge to it now.

The wall was directly in front of them, and the driver wasn't slowing down. In fact, he seemed to be speeding up as if he was going to—

Ember lurched back away from the driver. "Get down!" she screamed at the other passengers, then dropped to the floor herself and curled her arms around her head.

A second later, the trolley rammed into the wall.

Chapter Twenty-Two

For a long moment, Ember sat still, taking stock of herself. She'd smacked into something hard, perhaps a seat, at the impact, and she could feel a bruise starting to form on her left shoulder, but otherwise, she thought she was okay.

Slowly, mindful of the possibility of further injuries she couldn't feel yet, she lifted her head. She was facing the right side of the trolley now, and the passengers there were stirring. "Natalya?" a man whispered to the woman beside him who was bleeding a little from a cut on her cheek. "Are you all right?"

Ember looked toward the front of the trolley and gasped.

The entire front of the vehicle had been smashed flat against the giant ice wall, the driver pinned between his seat and the metal that made up the trolley's front. Even as he struggled to push himself free of the crash, he was muttering to himself, but his words, what Ember could make out, weren't words anymore, just a disconnected series of sounds without meaning.

But it wasn't just the trolley that had taken damage in the crash.

She hadn't noticed it at first, fixated as she was for a moment on the flailing, babbling trolley driver, but when she focused on the wall itself, she saw it: a crack.

Not just a crack, but nearly a hole.

And from that crack-that-was-almost-a-hole came blowing air.

Warm air.

It took a moment to register that, that the air coming from the other side of the wall was warm — Ember was having a hard time identifying the difference between the sensations touching her skin from the outside from the fear and confusion prickling her skin from the inside, but once she felt it, there was no mistaking it.

The air was warm. Warmer than the air inside any of the Frost buildings. Nearly warm like the air directly in front of a fire.

As the passengers on the trolley began, like her, to move from thinking about themselves and those immediately around them and look at what had happened, the tones of their voices began to change — from shaky and high from that initial adrenaline to something darker and much more afraid.

Ember stood, still slowly, still concerned about other injuries. She felt sore in several places, but nothing hurt sharply like something was broken, and her head mostly felt clear as understanding settled on her.

She stepped toward the driver doll. "Hey. You okay?"

His answer came out as a string of meaningless consonants.

Had something gotten jumbled in his speech programming? Ember wished she knew more about dolls than she did, wished she could do something other than deactivate them. She reached toward one of his hands, hoping to help him get free of the rubble around him, but even as she extended the gesture, the doll found the purchase on the trolley front he was apparently searching for. With a noise almost as loud and frightening as the crash itself, he shoved the mangled metal off his front and wormed his way out of his seat.

More noises came from his mouth, and while they still weren't stringing together into words, they had the tone all dolls adopted for their "the wall is cracking" refrain. The driver scrambled on torn hands and knees over the jagged bits of trolley and slid his fingers into the crack in the ice directly above the point of impact. His fingers seemed to sink almost through to the other side, and when he pulled, a chunk of ice came away with him.

"Get him down from there!" screamed another of the passengers from behind.

Footsteps shuffled forward, but Ember was too fixated on what was beyond the wall to notice.

Sand. From what she could tell, it seemed to be sand as far as the horizon, unbroken in every direction. The air wasn't just warm, but sweltering, and the wall around the hole made by the doll immediately began to drip with fresh melt.

Hands reached out past Ember, scrambling for any part of the doll, but he'd already squirmed his way through the hole and disappeared.

"Someone get the queen!" screamed that same voice from before, but no one else seemed especially inclined to move. Like Ember, most of them were staring, wide-eyed and slack-jawed, at the sand and heat on the other side of the wall.

The wall is cracking, Ember thought. No wonder.

The queen had been sure it was something wrong with

her machines that was doing it — some mechanical issue that she'd been sure Ember could fix.

But the wall wasn't cracking — it was *melting*.

"You." The screaming man prodded Ember's neighbor in the shoulder. His tone was still harsh, but the flailing panic of a moment before had been replaced with the tone of someone who was used to being obeyed. "Find an Envoy. We need to alert the queen at once. You" — he turned to another person on his left — "fetch some help."

Ember took a step toward the hole. If she could just get over the sharper bits of trolley remains, she might be able to pull herself through the wall—

"You! Get away from there!" The man's hand grabbed the back of her shirt and yanked her away from the hole. "Do you want to kill us all?"

"What's out there?" she asked, even though she knew the man wouldn't know — might even know less than she did. The air was still hot on her skin as it came through the hole, and the dripping around the edges had turned almost to a trickle. It would be a stream soon.

"It doesn't matter," the man grumbled. "Stay back."

As if she had a whole lot of options with him holding her by the shirt like that. Ember could've fought, perhaps, but the man wasn't threatening her — he kept glancing at the wall, at the stream of water sluicing off the edges of the hole, and his whole face was wracked with terror.

The roar of copter blades interrupted the other noises coming from the trolley passengers and the crowd that was beginning to form around them, and a moment later, the copter itself came thrumming into view. Everyone turned toward it, their terrified faces turned up like worshipers to their god, and murmurs of "The queen, the queen is here" rose beneath the other noises.

And indeed, as the copter set down, the blades spinning to a stop, the queen stood up from behind the driving levers and pushed open the door to the passenger bubble. "My dears, I need you all to look at me."

Everyone turned to her. The man holding Ember's shirt seemed to have forgotten her — his grip dropped away, and Ember was able to straighten the neck so it wasn't cutting into her throat.

She could guess at what was coming. The queen would make some kind of speech to calm the people around her, to whom she couldn't deny the truth of the hole, the warmth, the conspicuous not-end of the world beyond, then declare this section of town off-limits and pretend to the rest of the city that nothing had ever happened.

Ember wasn't interested in hearing it. With everyone focused on the soothing words of the queen, she might be able to slip out, maybe follow the driver doll.

Sand.

Those who said it spoke it like the name of a place, the way one said Dusk or Frost. But, like those places, Sand seemed to be named after some important feature of its surroundings.

If she could just get through the wall, she was sure she'd be well on her way to finding Sand. To finding the prince of Sand who was calling to the dolls.

A flash of color caught in the corner of her eye. Ember turned toward it, startled by the red in the usual pale colors of Frost.

Something sharp stuck into her neck. She had just enough time to wonder if she'd hurt herself worse than she initially thought, then everything went dark.

Chapter Twenty-Three

THERE WERE MONSTERS EVERYWHERE.

Ember couldn't quite see them — every time she turned, tried to look straight at them, they vanished into the empty white nothing around them. But she could feel them, pressing in, angry and hungry.

She woke with a gasp, sucking in air like she'd been holding her breath to the point of suffocation. Her head felt like it had been stuffed with mud, her thoughts thick and heavy and slow. Her mouth was dry, and her limbs ached.

She tried to sit up, to stretch her arms and legs, work the throbbing soreness out of her muscles, but she couldn't move. Something was wrapped around each wrist and ankle, and it took her a moment longer than it should've to identify it as rope.

"Ah. You're awake."

The voice floated toward her, pierced her aching head, equal parts familiar and threatening. Ember blinked, trying to force her eyes to focus, to stop seeing everything as monsters. The figure in front of her swam, edges leaking like the monsters in her dream, but the color, paired with the voice, allowed her to recognize it.

The queen.

Ember squirmed. The restraints around her wrists and ankles — rough, braided rope — bit into her skin. The places where it touched her burned, as if she'd already rubbed herself raw against it.

The queen took a step forward and placed a cool hand on Ember's hot forehead. "Be calm, *devushka*. I know it's a lot all at once, but you need to let yourself wake up gradually."

"You drugged me." Her voice scraped against her throat like fingernails.

"Not I."

"One of your people."

The queen smiled without humor. "Everyone inside Frost is 'my people.'"

"That's not what I meant."

"It's what you said, *devushka*. Perhaps you should learn to think before you speak." The queen's fingers moved slowly across Ember's forehead. The motion was gentle, motherly — sickening.

Ember jerked away. "Don't touch me."

The queen let her hand drop away but continued to smile that same empty smile. "My apologies."

"What do you want?"

"Well, then. To business, I suppose."

There was another chair placed in front of Ember's. The queen took it, crossed her legs at the ankles, and folded her hands on her lap. Normally, Ember wouldn't have noticed or cared how someone sat in a chair, but there was a deliberateness to every motion the queen made that made it hard to overlook. Everything she said, everything she did, even how she sat down, seemed to be filled with some kind of other unspoken purpose.

"You were on the trolley at the wall. Don't lie to me — I saw you there. It was where you were taken from."

Ember swallowed down a remark about how the queen couldn't read her quite as well as she thought. Ember had no intention of lying about that. She hadn't done anything wrong, after all — it was the doll, one of the queen's people, who'd driven the trolley into the wall and torn open the hole.

"I take it you saw what happened there?"

"Obviously," Ember said when the queen paused for an answer.

"This is what I was trying to prevent. Why I needed you to repair my machines."

"They aren't broken."

The queen was deadly quiet for a moment, and Ember wondered if she'd even heard her words. She tried again, a little louder.

"The machines aren't the problem. They aren't broken."

Still, though Ember was sure the queen must've heard, she didn't respond, just fixed Ember with a look that made Ember's skin prickle.

"Fix my machines, Ember Mikailanova."

"I can't. They aren't broken. Neither are the dolls. I think they might be getting instructions from somewhere—"

"That's not possible. The wall prevents it. The dolls only started malfunctioning when the wall began to crack. Fix my machines, and we'll solve all the problems in the city."

"But it's not the machines." Ember fought to keep her voice level, to not let it stretch up into her upset range. "It's the heat behind it that's making it crack. It's not malfunctioning — it's *melting*!"

The word sounded just as strange coming out of her mouth as it had echoing inside her head an hour or two before. But the truth of it was inescapable — she still felt the scorching heat of the air tingling against her skin, a phantom of warmth like she'd never felt before.

Of course a wall made of ice and snow was failing. The real wonder was how it had ever been built and maintained at all if that was what was pushing up against it.

The queen stood. She glanced toward one corner of the room, where an Envoy had stood, silent and staring off into the middle-distance, presumably since the queen had come into the room. "Fetch them."

The Envoy nodded once and left the room, but was back in another moment, this time trailing two more Envoys. Each held a knife and shoved in front of him a hooded figure with wrists bound behind their backs.

"What—?" Ember began but was interrupted when the new Envoys, almost as one, pulled the hoods off the heads of their captives.

Eli had clearly put up a struggle, had forced the Envoy to fight with him — both his eyes were ringed with bruises, his left eye swollen almost all the way shut, and his nose looked a little off-center from where it was the last time she'd seen him and was still bleeding freely down his chin and neck.

Felix hadn't gotten so roughed up — perhaps he'd gone willingly with whatever Envoy or doll that had fetched him — but fear and confusion shone like sunlight from his eyes. "Ember," he said softly. "What's going on?"

Ember wanted to get to her feet. Wanted to throw herself at the Envoys holding knives to her friends' throats. She'd probably take a drubbing herself, but it would be worth it if it got the threat of death away from them. But she couldn't move. The ropes bit harder against her skin as she pulled against them, tried to struggle her way free.

It was no use. She was trapped.

The queen stepped into Ember's line of sight, blocking most of her view of what was happening to the boys behind her. She was smiling again, and Ember was put in mind of a doll, always smiling whether it was warranted or not.

"Fix my machines, Ember Mikailanova, or you'll watch your friends die."

EMBER FOLLOWED the queen and Envoys through the hallways of the palace. She kept her steps light and even, determined not to give away anything more than she already had.

She couldn't launch herself at the Envoys, not while they had knives to her friends' throats. She didn't think the queen was bluffing when she said that she would have Eli and Felix killed in front of her if she didn't behave, and, even if she was, Ember wasn't willing to risk their lives on the chance that the queen wasn't being fully honest in her threat.

The hoods were back on their heads, and Felix in particular kept stumbling in his blindness. The Envoy holding him wasn't especially rough — perhaps he was one of Vallenovich's men, and maybe threatening the boss's son was a lot for him, even if it was on the order of the queen.

The Envoy holding Eli wasn't so tentative — he kept shoving at Eli as they walked, and he had the knife pointed out at Eli's throat, a proper threat rather than just a menacing prop. Ember noticed with no small satisfaction that his face was almost as bruised and bloody as Eli's; apparently Eli had gotten in a few solid hits before being subdued, and while that probably made him somewhat less charitable to his charge than the other man was, it still made Ember have to swallow her smile.

Of course Eli wouldn't take kindly to a kidnapping.

They ended up in a huge room full nearly to bursting with machines the size of buildings. Despite the fear and anger and confusion that ran through her veins, Ember couldn't help but marvel at the space.

"I assume I won't have to tell you again." The queen's voice cut through the near-deafening roar of the machines.

Ember grimaced back at her. The walk had helped to clear her head, but the noise still hurt worse than it ever had. Her head was throbbing, and that made it as hard to think as the drugs had.

She glanced over at her friends. Their hoods were still on, their hands bound, but she could still read the confusion in their stances, in the way both of them were turning their heads like they hoped to catch a glimpse of where they'd been brought. She wished she could talk to them, just for a second, just to let them know that she was working on a plan, some way to get them free.

They had to get to the copter. If they could just slip away from the room, get out of range of the Envoys' grasp, away from their knives, they could make it to the copter and fly over the wall.

Would the queen follow them? Ember didn't know. But it would be a lot harder to find them out in the sand beyond the wall, where people were afraid to go, than here in the city where everything was eventually reported back to her.

And perhaps the prince of Sand, whoever he was, wherever he was, would offer them a safe harbor.

So. That's what she had to do. Get Felix and Eli away from the Envoys long enough for them to slip off to the copter.

She just wished she could think of some way to do that.

The queen stepped into Ember's space, forcing her attention. She was still a strange and beautiful woman, even angry as she was, all pale skin and dark hair and blue edges. Atalanta as carved from ice. "You have an hour," she said, low enough that the words almost got lost in the rumble of the machines.

"I can't fix your machines," Ember tried once more, without any hope that it would be that simple but unable to resist. "There's nothing wrong with them. The wall is *melting*!"

The queen frowned, then turned toward her Envoys and nodded, a single commanding nod.

The man holding Eli jammed his knife into Eli's side.

"No!" Ember yelped and took a step toward him, but the queen grabbed her shirt and yanked her back.

"I'm not playing, *devushka*," she said. "You have an hour."

Blood stained the fabric of Eli's shirt. He tried to double over, but the Envoy's grip on his arms, the twist of his hands, forced him to remain upright. Ember's eyes burned with tears.

She yanked herself free of the queen's grip and turned toward the machines before the tears could fall in the queen's view.

I'm sorry, Eli, she thought, hard enough that she hoped he could at least sense it in the air around them. *I'm going to get us out of here.*

Whatever it took, she was going to get them all free.

The machines, monstrous as they were, were at least a soothing sight, well-made and sensible. She walked down them, watching pistons and belts until her sobs were under control, struggling to come up with something she could do, a plan.

It took her only a few minutes of looking over the roomful of machines to realize that she had no chance of understanding them, much less of a chance of fixing them. Buried inside the guts of one of the smallest, Ember felt her eyes fill and her throat close.

There was nothing she could do with these machines.

But she had to do *something*.

They had to get out of there.

A few of the machines had switches attached to them that powered down the whole thing when flipped. Ember flipped a switch on one of them and crawled underneath it to escape the queen's gaze.

It was better under the machine — the coils of metal, the gears and belts, the cooling warmth of kinetic energy and friction, made sense to her. Even though she knew there was nothing wrong with the machines, even though she knew that, even if there had been, it would be well outside of her own abilities to fix it, just being surrounded by things that made sense to her, away from the prying eyes of the queen and the horrifying view of Eli bleeding and Felix panicking, protected by innumerable tons of metal, was soothing. It helped to focus her thoughts and allowed her to *think*.

They had to get away from the Envoys. If they could do that, if there weren't knives threatening to snatch away her friends' lives, they would be okay. Ember could handle herself in a fight, Eli even wounded wouldn't back down, Felix knew how to dodge tails, and they'd be evenly matched. Three against three — or two, really, because Ember doubted the queen would insert herself into a physical brawl.

Those were decent odds.

It was the knives that were the problem.

Was there some way she could surprise the Envoys long enough for Felix and Eli to get out of range of their weapons? Something she could do to give her friends an advantage, even if momentarily?

Once again, she wished she could talk to them, even for a moment. Just a few words, a warning to be ready. Eli would understand. If Eli could get free, maybe together they could get Felix away safe.

Ember touched the stilled machine above her. These were the only weapons she had. If there was some way to use the machines to distract the Envoys...

It came to her then. It wasn't a great plan, or even a good one, but it was the only thing she'd thought of yet. It wouldn't work for more than a moment, and Felix and Eli wouldn't have any warning, but they were smart, and Eli at least ought to know that Ember was trying to get them free. He'd be ready.

She wiggled around in the guts of this machine. She didn't understand electricity all that well, but she could see how delicate all the internal workings of the machines were, could trace the electrical wires back to their source.

Ember squirmed her way out from underneath this machine and followed the wires back to a slightly smaller one that was running especially fast, producing the electricity that powered the one beside it. She allowed herself one quick glance toward the queen, who was watching her with pursed lips, then toward her friends, still hooded.

She didn't look at the blood smearing down Eli's side.

They'd have one chance, and the boys would have to be quick without any warning, but it was the best she could do.

Ember made her way around the side of the electricity

machine. Belts and gears whirred, pistons pumped. For a single moment, she let herself appreciate the properly working order of the whole thing. Then she closed her eyes tight against the light, hoping that would force her eyes to adjust to the darkness before it happened. With her fingertips, she groped around a bit of the metal plating, found a loose bolt, and, squinting open only one eye so as not to lose too much of that adjustment to darkness, dropped it into the gears.

The gears ground to a halt, and the lights in the room flashed off.

Chapter Twenty-Four

MOVEMENT. Feet shuffling, voices yelling. Ember darted out from between the machines. The darkness was almost complete, the only light coming from the closed door into the hallway, where presumably a torch still flickered, and even prepared for it, she was momentarily blinded by it.

No matter. She knew where the Envoys were standing, and even without being able to see too well, she could make out the motion from the shadows that suggested Eli and Felix had indeed noticed and taken advantage of their sudden distraction.

She launched herself at the Envoy holding Eli, who was a step closer than the other. He stumbled backwards, unprepared for her attack, and she wrenched the knife out of his hands before he could regain his balance.

"Eli," she hissed.

"Here," he answered, his voice tight with pain.

She pulled the hood off his head and sliced through the rope binding his hands. "Run!"

He staggered forward, one hand at his wounded side, out of reach of the Envoy.

She turned toward the other to find Felix already out of his bonds and yanking the hood off his own head. His Envoy was doubled over a step behind him, one hand over his face and the other wrapped around his middle.

So. The Frost boy could put up a fight. In any other circumstance, Ember might have to take a moment to be impressed — as it was, now was not the time.

Felix grabbed her arm. In the other hand, he held his own captor's knife. Both of them took off after Eli.

"They're running!" the queen screeched. "Don't let them get away!"

They caught up to Eli, and even in the dark, Ember could see pain lacing every inch of him, from the sweat on his brow to the uncertain placement of his feet. She grabbed his arm and pulled it around her shoulders. He winced but leaned a little of his weight against her, allowing her to pull him along faster than he could run on his own.

Footsteps pounded behind them. Only one set for now, probably the Envoy who'd had Eli, but she didn't doubt that the other would join him soon. She glanced at Felix. "We need to lose the tail. Get to the copter."

Felix half-grinned. "Follow me."

He led them through the machines, weaving in and out between them like he did on the streets when they were dodging a tail. The lights hadn't come back on — Ember wasn't sure if they would, if she'd condemned all of Frost to the dim world of only natural light and fires.

The thought pinged like regret inside her — she shook it off before that could stop her feet.

Felix took a sharp left, bringing them full around one of the machines so they were nearly back to where they'd started, but the Envoys were still chasing them, following their trail instead of trying to cut them off. Only the queen stood between them and the door out of the room, and stood she did, with her spine straight and her eyes flaming.

"Felix, isn't it?" the queen said, her voice low and soothing, her eyes fixed on him as the person mostly likely susceptible to her words. "You're Dmitri's son."

Felix froze, suddenly blocking their way almost as effectively as the queen was. He'd never been anything but profoundly worshipful of the queen, and now Ember could see the fear and confusion and uncertainty play across his face.

The Envoys had stopped running after them and were now coming up slow and quiet like they hoped the queen would be sufficient distraction for them to jump them from behind.

"What are you doing, Felix? It isn't right for you to throw in your lot with these dangerous outworlders." The queen held out a hand toward him. "I think you want to be home now. You would be if your Dusk friends would just cooperate."

The Envoys were closing in. Ember tightened her grip on the knife. She didn't want to fight, and certainly not with a knife, but she would if she had to.

But if the queen turned Felix on them, it would go from three against three to four against two, and one of those four would be her friend. The Frost boy she'd trusted, the one she liked in a way that was different even than the way she liked Eli.

Perhaps, she even liked him in a way she could never like Eli.

Could she put her hands on him, hurt him, even in a fight? She wasn't sure.

Felix tore his eyes off the queen, met Ember's, and something in his expression changed, solidified. That switch Ember had seen toggled off and on before disappeared, and Ember understood.

He was with her. He wasn't a Frost boy, one of the queen's people, anymore.

And, if that expression wasn't enough to prove it, a moment later, he whirled back to the queen and punched her in the nose.

EMBER DIDN'T RECOGNIZE this part of Frost, but Felix moved confidently through the darkened streets, so she followed him. Eli was growing heavier and heavier at her side, but he only nodded when she asked if he was okay, if he could keep going.

They'd come out of the machine room into what, from the domed roofs and colorful, faded bricks, looked to be somewhere in the old city, though currently the cathedral wasn't visible in the narrow, twisting streets. The lights on the street were all out, and the hum of a crowd was just audible over the pounding of their feet.

"Felix," Ember gasped after a couple of blocks. "I think we've lost them."

He slowed but didn't look at her. His jaw was set, his eyes staring straight forward, as if looking around would reveal to him what he'd done.

She wanted to reach out to him. Take his hand. Maybe pull him into her arms. Tell him that he'd done the right thing. That he wasn't the queen's property, not a doll, not one of her playthings. He had every right to choose who he sided with and let that choice be known in no uncertain terms.

That he'd saved them. Striking the queen, making his choice so inarguably known, so uncontestably decided, wasn't wrong.

But Ember didn't have a free hand to offer him — one was holding up Eli, the other was wrapped around a knife turning rusty with dried blood.

Later, she promised herself. Once they were over the wall, out of the queen's grip. Once Eli didn't need her to lean on, she'd reach out to Felix and tell him every one of those things.

For now, they needed to get to the copter.

"Where are we?" she asked at last as their run slowed to a walk, their escape turned to seeking a destination.

Felix looked around a little, though not at Ember or Eli, squinting through the dark at one unlit electric light. "The old city. The cathedral's this way."

He started forward again, not running anymore to avoid attracting attention, but with a firmness and direction to his pace that suggested he knew exactly where they were and how to get to where they were going.

Ember, unfamiliar with the old city beyond the path from the Queen's Line to the cathedral, was happy enough to follow.

"Hold on, Eli," she whispered. "We'll get to the copter, and then we'll be free."

"I'm fine," Eli gritted out, but his face was pale and his skin was clammy.

Ember held him a little tighter and picked up their pace.

They met a crowd after the third turn. Much like the people at the trolley accident, everyone looked confused and frightened, speaking over each other or sobbing softly to themselves. "Where's the queen? Why has her magic failed?" they asked.

Ember couldn't see any dolls in the crowd — a first for an assortment of Frost citizens. Had they all gone mad like the trolley driver and the others she'd deactivated? Had they all slipped through the wall and out into the desert beyond?

One woman noticed them first and shrieked above the sounds of the others. "Outworlders!"

Ember froze. The word, usually a neutral one coming from a Frost citizen, was spoken like a slur — sharp and angry and afraid.

The crowd turned toward them, pressed in with sudden and unusual aggression, the veneer of friendly disinterest gone. "You!" someone else yelled. "You've ruined our city!"

"You've destroyed our queen!"

"Nothing's wrong with the queen," Ember tried. "She's fine. It's the machine that broke!"

But no one was listening to her. They pressed in, and the tone of their hums were growing from afraid to enraged.

Ember had never actually been in a serious fight. She could hold her own against one opponent, and she had always kept a knife nearby if she was leaving her house because of the risk of being attacked in the streets, but once she'd gotten in a few good licks and pulled out a knife, every person who'd tried to attack her before had realized she wasn't going to be the easy pickings they'd hoped for and left her alone without any need for her to put her knife anywhere serious.

But people of Dusk didn't trust each other enough to gang up on a single person, and everyone knew everyone else's reputation. After a few broken noses, shallow knife cuts, and Eli's insistence that Ember was his, Ember's reputation was well-known enough that she didn't get into many scraps, and for the most part, she was left alone.

So looking at a crowd of people with murder in their

panicking eyes was more than Ember knew what to do with.

She readjusted her grip on her knife and tried to think through the descending panic. Arms, legs, sides were all places a knife could go and do enough damage to halt a person in their tracks without necessarily killing them.

She'd never wished more for dolls. At least she knew how to handle dolls.

Eli shifted, too, pulling away from Ember's hold and straightening. His breath hitched, and pain was written in the tightness of his jaw, but Ember recognized the stubbornness in his face.

Neither of them was going to go down without a fight. They were Dusk folk, after all — too stubborn to die.

Felix stepped a little to one side, so he was standing directly in front of Ember and Eli, his arms spread in a stance as much protective as pleading. "Just let us go," he said, and his voice was strangely level, the only hint of fear coming from the way his fingers had closed into fists. "We're leaving, and we won't bother you again."

"Traitor!"

And with that declaration, the mob descended.

Ember didn't have time to be careful about where her knife hit — people came at her fast and furious, and she had to move equally fast. They were out to kill her and Eli and Felix. She couldn't allow herself to be shy about trying to kill them back.

She jammed the knife into whatever part she could reach of the man who first came at her, his hands in fists and raised for a strike. It was his forearm as it came down at her face, and the knife took the brunt of his force. He howled in pain and rage and tore his arm away, the motion opening the wound up further and spraying Ember's face and chest with blood. He staggered back a step, still screaming, and looked down at the wound.

"Dirty bitch!"

She was about to answer, to ask him to stop, leave her and her friends alone, when someone else struck her from the side.

The pain of the blow was startling, a fist across her left cheek making her gasp for her next breath. She whirled around, jabbing blindly with her knife, and felt the metal meet skin once more.

This time, it hit the person's neck.

The attacker, a woman, gagged, open-mouthed and unable to pull in air. Ember pulled away, horrified, her whole body going numb, the realization of what she'd just done catching up with her as the woman dropped to her knees, one hand at her sliced-open throat.

She bumped against another person and started to turn on them, too, but it was Eli. He grabbed her arm and pulled her away from the dying woman, toward an open path out of the mob. "Run!" he hissed at her. "I'll watch our backs."

She didn't need to be told twice.

She caught up to Felix in a couple of strides, where he'd already broken through the mob, and sprinted after him. Eli took up the rear, watching their backs as he'd promised, but the mob, for all its anger, didn't seem especially interested in following. One person yelled that they were getting away, but maybe more people were as stunned by the woman dying in front of them as Ember was, or maybe they, like many men in Dusk, weren't interested in anyone who fought back.

It didn't matter. Whatever the reason, Ember was just glad that the mob didn't follow.

They wove through the streets, blinded by darkness and

panic, dodging around people whenever they could and shoving past them whenever they couldn't. Mostly the people they met outside that initial mob were too caught up in their own fear to notice or care about the outworlders and the Frost boy running for their lives covered in their own or others' blood, and Ember said a grateful prayer to Mother Atalanta for that, for the fact that they weren't stopped again.

They crashed through the doors of the cathedral at last and dropped hard into the repaired copter.

ELI SLUMPED into the glass bottom of the copter's passenger bubble. His side was bleeding freely, and the blood that had coated his lips and neck was running fresh again. He coughed weakly, then winced as the motion pulled at the knife wound in his side.

Ember wanted to slump down with him, but there wasn't time. If the queen hadn't rallied yet, she would soon, and the presence of the queen telling Frost to get them would re-inflame the mobs. She might even be coming with her own copter, intent on chasing them down or heading them off.

They had to get out of the city. Over the wall. On their way to Sand, wherever that was.

Ember didn't know if it would be safer there, but it couldn't possibly be any more dangerous.

"See if you can stop the bleeding," she said, probably to Felix, but she didn't check if he heard her, only trusted that he had and made her way to the controls of the copter.

She'd been practicing as best she could for the last couple of days, but that didn't make her feel any more capable as she flipped the switches and turned on the blades.

The copter's blades began to rotate, slowly at first, but quickly gathering speed, until she could feel the lift beginning to lighten the weight on the runners. She nudged the lever to tilt the front blades, and the whole thing lifted straight off the ground.

"Hold on, boys. We're flying."

She turned the lever, and the copter spun toward the door. With another nudge forward, it burst out of the cathedral.

Some people had followed them — several folks had to duck away from the copter as it crashed against the doors, too low and unprepared yet for getting higher. Ember gritted her teeth and held the levers with both hands, trying to ignore the way the sweat on her palms made her grip slippery and the thundering of her heart nearly drowned out the roar of copter blades.

Higher. She had to get higher, or she'd end up crashing them straight into the next building.

She pulled on the lever that gave them height, and the copter jerked up so fast that her stomach couldn't keep up and she nearly got sick across her controls — only her clenched-tight jaw kept the bile and acid from her stomach from spilling out her mouth.

Eli coughed again, and the sound was wet, like there was blood in it now.

"Ember," Felix said weakly.

"Don't you give up on me now. Not either of you, hear? We're going over this damned wall, and no one's going to stop us."

She banked hard to the right. South — the direction her manufactured compass, which she mounted onto the copter's dash, had been urging her to go ever since it started malfunctioning.

She was sure now that it was all connected. Whatever had disrupted the dolls, whatever had sparked the melting of the wall, caused the earthquake, misaligned her compass, even provoked her dreams of some great and terrible engine — it was all the same thing. It was pulling at her, and now, finally, she was going to *find it*.

They rushed through the city, gaining air as the copter settled into its flight speed, brushing over the tops of even the tallest buildings Frost could build, until at last the wall rose before them, as tall and impenetrable as it had ever been.

Except it wasn't. It was melting, and there was warmth on the other side. It could be cracked by a trolley and torn through by a doll. It was as fragile as ice in front of a fire, and the queen of Frost had done everything she could to keep her people from knowing that.

No more.

Ember adjusted her grip on the copter's controls. "Hold on," she said again. "We're going through."

Something huge and black emerged from the corner of Ember's vision. She looked at it with just her eyes, not turning her head, and saw the queen in her own copter coming up beside them.

"Ember," she said, her voice magnified over the sounds of two copters and tinny in a way Ember didn't recognize. "You don't understand what you're doing. If you go over this wall, you'll doom us all. Not just me, but yourself, your friends, everyone who's managed to scrape together a life after the Leshii died."

Ember couldn't talk back to her — whatever device she had in her copter to make herself audible, Ember didn't have it.

But it didn't matter. She was saying those things to try and stop her, but Ember wasn't going to be stopped.

They were lies. Everything the queen of Frost said was a lie, and Ember should've known that right from the start.

For the first time, Ember looked back at her passengers. Eli was sitting half-propped against the curve of the glass bubble, Felix beside him pressing a wadded-up piece of cloth to his injured side. Both of them were bloody and bruised, their clothing tattered even where Felix hadn't torn off several inches at the bottom of his pants to help stem the flow of Eli's blood, and Ember's heart ached.

She'd dragged them into this. If not for her, neither of them would be in such a state.

But they both looked up when she turned back to them. Eli pushed himself up a bit against the wall, and Felix nodded.

"Do it," he said, and she knew they were both with her, just as they'd been the whole time.

Ember jammed the steering lever forward, and the copter smashed against the wall, shattering the fragile ice with iron blades.

Chapter Twenty-Five

THEY FLEW FOR HOURS, and there was still nothing but barren desert on every horizon.

Ember had finally set the copter down on a flat piece of land, too exhausted to keep concentrating on flying the machine, and let the world grow dark around them.

The heat was stifling. She'd never felt anything like it. It sucked the moisture out of her mouth and the sweat off her brow, and now, several hours after leaving the cool of Frost, she felt wrinkled and small and delirious.

The boys didn't seem to be in better shape. Eli's eyes had closed some time ago, and now he lay crumpled on the floor, raspy breaths and sluggish bleeding the only indication that he was still alive. Felix sat curled up in the very back, his legs against his chest and his arms wrapped around his knees, rocking very slightly back and forth and whispering to himself words Ember couldn't quite make out.

Despite her exhaustion, the heat that weighed on her shoulders and headache that pounded at her bruised skull, Ember couldn't relax. The complete featureless desert wasn't unlike the tundra in the fact that its lack of shelter and extreme temperature promised death to anyone who didn't keep their wits about them, and she was apparently the only one with wits left to keep.

But the pressure, the heat, the strangeness of it all, kept her knife in her hand and her restless, panicked energy on a hair trigger.

"What was that?" Felix asked suddenly, straightening out of the ball he'd curled himself into.

Ember turned. She couldn't see anything through the dusty glass of the copter but sand and more sand, distinguished from the scattering of rocks only by the way the hot wind collected and spun it around.

She couldn't see or hear anything else.

"I thought I saw…" Felix's voice trailed off. He bit his lip. "Maybe not. Just a shadow."

"I don't like this," Ember admitted, mostly so she wouldn't have to keep thinking the words only to herself.

"Yeah. Maybe we should keep flying?"

"I'm worried about the fuel. I'd rather—" She choked on her words, cleared her throat, tried again. "Rather we fly during the day, when we can see, and preserve the fuel at night. I'm not sure how long a copter can go on only one tank."

"Right. That's smart." But he didn't sound convinced.

Neither did she, really, because it wasn't much of a plan, and they both knew that. None of her ideas had been much of a plan, not since first deciding to go with Eli to Frost. Everything had been reaction, and the plans she formed had only been thought through to the point where they got her over the wall and out of Frost.

They'd been over the wall for hours, and now, Ember felt like it might've been the stupidest idea she'd ever had. At least in Frost they had food and water and shelter.

"Don't." Felix's voice interrupted the dour turn of her thoughts.

"Don't what?"

"Don't go regretting it. It was right. The queen lied. About everything. And she needed to be exposed for that."

"Yeah. I know." Now she was the one who sounded unconvinced.

Felix scooted forward, careful not to bump Eli and disturb what was probably not a particularly healing sleep, but was at least something to help him dull the pain. He propped himself up onto his knees and set one rusty hand on her leg. "Ember, look at me."

She did, slowly.

He looked back at her with perfect seriousness. "I don't regret it. Neither should you. Whatever happens, we're in this together, right?"

She put her free hand over his, laced their fingers together. "Right."

He smiled, just a little, with just the corners of his lips, but it felt so good to see his smile that Ember couldn't help but smile back.

Then, slowly, making sure it was okay with every shift she made, she tilted toward him, lowered her head against his shoulder, and finally let her eyes slip shut.

"EMBER MIKAILANOVA."

The sound of her name jolted through the drowsy almost-peace that had settled on her. Ember jerked upright and spun around, knife lifted, prepared to kill again if she had to.

There was a man standing outside the now-opened door of the copter's passenger bubble. He was swathed from head to toe in light, loose cloth, only the shine of his eyes visible from between a head wrap and a face covering, and he held a small black tube that shone a powerful electric light out of one end.

"It's okay," he said, lifting his cloth-covered hands as if to prove he wasn't armed. "I'm a friend. The prince of Sand has sent me to fetch you."

Ember's story continues...

Prince of Sand, Book 2 of *The Frost Trilogy* is a thrilling journey beyond the southern wall to the city of Sand where Ember will face the question, what is she willing to sacrifice to find the truth and save the world?

Get Prince of Sand today!

A Note From The Author

If you enjoyed this book, please take a moment to write a short review on your favorite online bookstore so other readers can enjoy it, too.

Thanks so much!
Aria Noble

About the Author

Aria Noble tells stories of ordinary girls thrust into extraordinary worlds full of mysteries and magic. Her characters aren't afraid to question their assumptions, discover their strength, and possibly even change the world along the way. Fans of Shannon Hale, Phillip Pullman, and Marissa Meyer will love Aria Noble.

Also By Aria Noble

The Frost Trilogy

Queen of Frost

The Prince of Sand

Lady of Dawn

Stand-Alone Novels

Alien Fairytales: The Complete Collection

www.ingramcontent.com/pod-product-compliance
Lightning Source LLC
Chambersburg PA
CBHW010542100726
47903CB00011B/3100